ORIGINS

ORIGINS

THE MISSING LINK TRILOGY
BOOK THREE

Kate Thompson

BLOOMSBURY

Published by Bloomsbury U.S.A. Children's Books
175 Fifth Avenue, New York, NY 10010
Distributed to the trade by Holtzbrinck Publishers

Library of Congress Cataloging-in-Publication Data
Thompson, Kate.
Origins / by Kate Thompson. — 1st U.S. ed.
p.   cm. — (Missing link trilogy ; bk. 3)
Summary: Christy's souvenir stone from the yeti's cave proves to be fatal
for many of the inhabitants of Fourth World leaving among the survivors a
pair of genetically-altered twins whose eventual descendants face an
uncertain future in a stone age world of nuclear devastation and disease.
ISBN-13: 978-1-58234-652-6 • ISBN-10: 1-58234-652-6 (alk. paper)
[1. Genetic engineering—Fiction. 2. Future life—Fiction.
3. Animals—Fiction. 4. Science fiction.] I. Title.
PZ7.T3715795Ori 2007   [Fic]—dc22   2007006924

Typeset by Hewer Text UK Ltd, Edinburgh
Printed in the U.S.A. by Quebecor World Fairfield
1 3 5 7 9 10 8 6 4 2

For Sophie

part
one

There wasn't a breath of wind. In the woods a perfect stillness governed the gathering darkness. If there were other hunters abroad in the night, they were lying as low as Nessa was. Like her, they were no strangers to patience. She waited.

High above her in the colossal oak two fat pigeons were sleeping. Nessa could neither see them nor hear them, but she had located them as they flew in to roost at dusk. Their position in the tree was fixed clearly in her mind. She would have no trouble finding them.

A leaf dropped from the branches above and landed on her foot. Another fell nearby, and then another, as though the tree had sensed the sudden end of summer and had begun to withdraw its energy back into its ancient heart, abandoning its extremities to their annual death. For an instant Nessa wished she could do something similar; retreat to some warm, safe place and go into hibernation. Through the foliage a few bright stars were glinting. There would be long, cold nights ahead and long, cold, lonely days.

Nessa stood up, warding off the chilling thoughts with action.

No Cat need ever fear to walk alone . . .

Before she began to climb, she collected herself, as she had been taught.

I come to you, father, as clean as on the day I was born.
These four things I ask of you.
Clear sight, to win the friendship of darkness.
Patience, to win the friendship of time.
Stillness, to win the friendship of action.
Courage, to win the friendship of death.
These four skills Atticus, our father, has given us.
Praise him.

Tuesday ~~Thursday~~: February 5

This diary was a brilliant birthday present from Maggie. My birthday was three months ago, but she could hardly give it to me then, so she saved it for when I got back from Tibet. It's years out of date, but I don't care. I'd say it's almost impossible to get hold of a current one, and as long as I can get the day right I don't care about the year.

Maggie said I should write down all our adventures in it. Trouble is, it would take me too long. So many things have happened since Darling the starling arrived on my windowsill to escort me and my goofy stepbrother, Danny, here to Fourth World in the north of Scotland. Where would I start?

It's funny, the way your mind works. When Darling first spoke to me, I thought it was a dream or something, and then when we met up with Oggy the dog, and he talked too, I thought it was some kind of magic. It never occurred to me that it could have a scientific basis, but that's what it turned out to be. It wasn't until we got here to Fourth World that I found out about the 'missing link' - the gene for language which Bernard and Maggie had isolated and put into various animals and birds. Before that, they were involved in some other, more dubious experiments which involved putting animal genes into their own children. That was why Danny's behaviour had seemed so weird. He has dolphin genes. His half-sister, Sandy, has frog genes, which make her incredibly strong, and Colin, the youngest of the kids here at Fourth World, has the anti-freeze gene from the salmon, which means he can survive sub-zero temperatures. Lucky for him, as it turned out, since he got buried in an avalanche in Tibet and wouldn't be here at all if it wasn't for his DNA.

That was during another recent adventure, when some of us went off in search of the yeti because Bernard wanted to find out if it really existed and, if it did, whether or not it had the missing link gene.

(Decided to use a loose sheet of paper and stick it in, instead of spilling over into tomorrow. Klaus, the pink mouse, has gone tearing off to find me a paper-clip).

I don't think any of us really expected to find a yeti, but we did. She was the last of her kind, living alone up there at the top of the world. She told us the story of her race; how they were the original intelligent species and how one branch of her ancient ancestors took to the sea and became merfolk, and how our own species, mankind, developed when some of them came back from the sea and recolonised the land. We have every reason to believe that it's true, because Danny met the merfolk - got kidnapped by them, in fact, when we were on our sea voyage to the Bay of Bengal.

But nobody, not even the yeti, has been able to answer the fundamental question that underlies all Bernard and Maggie's experiments and research. Where did the missing link gene originate?

It seems now as if there isn't anywhere else for us to look. And if that's the case, then the chances are that nobody will ever know.

W hen Nessa had eaten, she went to the mossy spring nearby, washed herself scrupulously, and offered a short prayer of thanks for the meal. Afterwards, free of the taint of pigeon blood, she stood quietly and made a thorough scenting of the night. There was a badger nearby; aware of her presence and keeping as still as she was. There were faint traces of grunt as well, but not recent; it was probably two or three days since they had passed this way. Another smell, of freshly opened acorns, caught her attention and she followed it to its origin in a tiny hollow beneath the roots of a hawthorn.

She kneeled down and peered in. There were mice in there; she could smell their fear as they huddled in the darkness, smelling her too, and listening to her soft breathing. On another night she might have hunted them for sport, exercising her patience and testing the speed of her reactions. But tonight she had no heart for it. There was no point, since there would be no returning to the village and offering the tiny gifts to her young cousins.

The thought produced a jolt of dread. Nessa left the mice in peace and moved rapidly through the darkness until she came to a pile of jumbled stones at the bottom of a scrubby slope. Before she left she had promised to visit that spot each morning at dawn. If and when it was considered safe for her to return to the village someone would come and meet her there.

It was much too early, she knew. She also knew that she

should spend as little time as possible there, in case the place began to take on her scent. If anyone was out hunting for her they might come to suspect her movements and lay a trap. A short distance away she stopped and took another reading of the night air. Her nose and her ears told her it was safe. There were no enemies there. No friends, either.

Perhaps someone would come at dawn. Surely they would. How many nights had it been, now? Six? Seven? More? They wouldn't leave her much longer, would they? It had to be safe by now. Unless . . .

Nessa crouched among the stones and listened to the night. A few trees away an owl called, and a second one answered from across the forest.

No Cat need ever fear the moon's dominion.
Atticus has told us this.
Praise him.
No Cat need ever fear to walk alone.
Atticus has told us this.
Praise him.
No enemy shall overcome the spirit of the
    fighting Cat.
Atticus protects his own.
Praise him.

But if Atticus had protected his children in Nessa's village, where were they? Why had no one come to fetch her back?

The thought was sacrilegious. Nessa clutched the icon around her neck and raised her eyes to the black sky. This time she spoke the words aloud:

'No Cat need ever fear the moon's dominion . . .'

Wary of staying in one place for too long, Nessa left the stones and wandered through the woods. She wasn't hungry.

Under normal circumstances that would not have stopped her from hunting, but this night was different. She had no heart for the chase.

As dawn began to break she washed again, then returned to the stones. No one was there. No one had been there.

Nessa didn't wait. She walked away, climbing the escarpment above the rockfall, looking for a safe place to sleep. On previous days she had gone for several miles before choosing a tree with branches stout enough to make a reasonable bed, but that morning her spirits were too low. She had no energy for more walking. She knew it was risky and, worse than that, she knew that lack of interest in her own welfare was a dangerous sign. Any creature that loses sight of the value of its own life will soon become an easy target for hunters.

Halfway up the slope was a sheer wall of rock; not high, but well above the reach of a hound. To get onto it Nessa shinned up a tree and leaped from its reaching branches onto the top of the rock. There was a nice grassy perch up there, unsheltered from any rain that might fall, but offering an excellent view of the forest floor below. Nessa turned around in it a few times and closed her eyes experimentally. It felt safe.

She lay down, wrapped her sheepskin around her shoulders and tucked her hands beneath her armpits. Before long her limbs were warm, but not even the cherished skin could keep the growing chill from her heart. What had happened? Why had no one come? To begin with Nessa had been anxious, but no more than that. She had been sure that the troubles in the village would be resolved. The wise uncles and aunts would sort it out. The troublemakers would be brought to book; might even be handed over to the other side to face the consequences of their crime. Everything would be all right. But with each day that passed it looked worse.

Nessa turned over, trying to move her attention away from the gloomy thoughts. If she hadn't been forbidden to return, she would have faced any danger rather than stay in that unknown place, alone. She fingered the carved icon on its leather thong.

Atticus preserve me and all who belong to me.

All who belonged to her had been in the village. Had he preserved them?

Nessa turned back to face the trees again. A blackbird was singing heartily in a branch a few feet away from her face. Every morning of her life she had drifted off to sleep in the village trees, surrounded by birdsong. It was her lullaby. But now, her peace of mind disturbed by worry, she found the blackbird's song an irritation.

She sat up. A spear of light from the rising sun pierced the branches and caught her full in the eye. She felt the sharp, almost painful contraction as her pupils narrowed rapidly. Instinctively she turned to look into the shadows. Her gaze rested more comfortably there, but she could not ignore the unpleasant reminder of why she was there; isolated by the thing that set her apart from the other members of her community. She was the special one; one of the Watchers. Whatever happened to the rest of her community, she must be kept safe. And as every Cat knew, the safest place in the world was in the forest, alone. In the loving, protecting arms of Atticus.

Wednesday ~~Friday~~: February 6

I had an awful dream last night. I dreamed I was up on top of the world with the yeti, except that the top of the world wasn't the Himalayas, it was the side of the glen here, up above the windmills. We were looking down at the whole planet, somehow, and it was completely silent. There was nobody alive down there at all, and I had this thought - that the missing link gene had never existed. It was a dream that me and the yeti had dreamed together.

It doesn't sound too bad now I've written it down, but it frightened me witless. I was rigid with fear when I woke up.

The latest news is that Electra, one of the first of the talking cats, has had four kittens. The father, she tells us, was a gentleman from the village. He didn't talk, of course, but the kittens will, because they'll get the ability from their mother. It's great when the young animals first start talking. I can't wait.

There will be more soon, as well. Loki is not far off having her pups.

I don't know why I'm writing all this. I should be sleeping. I'm useless in the mornings these days because I can't sleep when I go to bed at night, no matter how late it is. I'm uneasy the whole time. I have this awful feeling that something's going to happen. It could be the fear that we'll get invaded again. Those guys were really brutal; they did terrible things to the animals and they wrecked the place. So I am nervous about it happening again, but I don't think that's the reason I can't sleep. I think it's because of the stone the yeti gave me up in her cave in the Himalayas. I haven't shown it to anybody yet. It's a kind of guilty secret. I don't know why I don't want to tell anyone. I don't even want to take it out and look at it myself. But I'm always aware of it there under my mattress. It's always on my mind when I'm trying to get to sleep. It's just an old stone, an axe-head or something, but it meant such a lot to the yeti. She trusted me with it. I don't feel worthy of that trust.

I wish I knew what to do.

The roots of the conflict went too far back in time to be understood. All Nessa knew was that Cats and Dogs were different. Always had been. Always would be. Dogs, she had been taught, were dirty and cowardly. They did not wash. They hunted in daylight, in groups, with packs of hounds, and they feared the night. They worshipped a false god, whose name was Ogden. They were deaf and blind to the truth of the one and only true god, whose name was Atticus.

Her bile rose and the hairs on the back of her neck stiffened. She had always known that Dogs were the enemy. How was it that she and all of her kin had become blind to the fact?

Throughout her life the two communities had been at peace, side by side. The eldest residents remembered the last war, but they had succeeded in putting their grievances behind them and lived in peaceful co-existence. Even the smallest cousin knew the dreadful history of the ancient rivalry, but it seemed to be a thing of the past. There was plenty of room for everyone. The Dogs were herders: they kept cattle and sheep, preferring the open spaces of meadow and farmland to the dark forests where the Cats hunted and gathered and followed their less regimented lifestyles. In the marketplace there were no ethnic divides. Cats traded their forest products – firewood, pelts and game – for the farm produce of the Dogs. Each community had its own skills. Some of the specialisation was bizarre. Cats didn't use much in the way of furniture, but their gifted carpenters made tables, chairs and cupboards for the Dog community. And the Dogs, though they never cut their own hair, produced the fine tools needed to keep the Cats' hair and beards neatly trimmed, as well as the barbers who used them.

The current conflict had small, almost insignificant beginnings. A scrubby area on the edge of some Cat-controlled woodland was cleared by a party of Dogs during daylight hours, when there were no Cats around to see what they were doing. The Cats complained, claiming that the land was part of the forest and not, as the farmers contended, meadowland that had become overgrown due to neglect. A meeting was held by a pair of respected elders from each community, and the verdict that was reached went in favour of the Cats. If the Dogs had neglected their land long enough for the forest to encroach upon it, they could not be deemed to have real need of it. The guilty parties were ordered to replant the trees they had felled and to protect them from their cattle. To all intents and purposes, the dispute was settled.

But it didn't end there. The wall that was built around the woodland proved inadequate. The cattle broke in again and destroyed the young trees.

It had always been acknowledged that cattle which wandered into the forest were fair game for Cats, but under normal conditions, in expression of goodwill for their neighbours, the Cat practice was to return straying beasts to safe enclosures. But on this occasion there was no goodwill on offer. The Cats who came across those cattle slaughtered them and, as an expression of contempt, left the carcasses where they lay.

The disputed woodland was a short distance from Nessa's home. She had been among the first to see the carcasses, on her return from a satisfying night's hunting in the forest nearby. The image remained with her and still filled her with dread. She lived on fresh meat and a night rarely passed without her hunting down and killing some creature or other, but she had never seen wanton slaughter before. The strewn carcasses seemed like a representation of something much more sinister; a reminder of the ancient animosities between the communities. A portent.

She knew that she was not the only one who thought so. Throughout the following days an anxious mood infected the atmosphere. Though no one said it aloud, it was well known to her and everyone else in the village who had killed those beasts. Every community has its warriors, whether they are required or not.

Passions became inflamed. It was possible that the cattle had broken down the wall themselves, but no one chose to believe that. The Cats accused the Dogs of knocking it down, and the Dogs accused the Cats of doing it themselves. Neither side was prepared to dispose of the carcasses. The Cats said it was the responsibility of the Dogs who owned them. The Dogs said that since they were straying and therefore legitimate game, it was up to the hunters to remove the kill. The dead cattle rotted where they lay. Before long the stench of decay reached the village and made life even more miserable for the anxious inhabitants. Tensions between the communities increased. Encounters in the market and on the common footpaths often turned into arguments, quarrels, even scuffles. Trade relations began to break down. And, as had happened countless times in the past, the few reckless self-appointed warriors on each side began to gather recruits.

Grand-aunts and grand-uncles from Nessa's village met with elders from the Dogs, and a peace plan was formulated. A party composed of members of both communities would gather on the disputed land and bury the cattle. After that, to prevent further incursions, guards would be posted along both sides of the wall until the situation settled down.

But the plan was stillborn. Before it could be put into

action, extremist elements of the Cat community carried out a plan of their own. In the dead of night, while she was returning home, her pocket full of wriggling mice so the young cousins could practise their hunting skills, Nessa encountered a gang from her village holding a meeting in a tree. She could tell by the scent of them that they were all recently washed, which in itself was suspicious. They were also highly excited, whispering and posturing among themselves. There was no doubt in Nessa's mind about what it meant. Trouble.

She joined them in the tree, even though they made it clear that she was not in the least bit welcome. She knew that they had been trying to stir up trouble ever since the cattle first broke into the forest. Some of the uncles had already taken them aside and talked to them about the need for calm, but it had clearly had no effect. They had been taught, after all, that the Dogs were their enemy, even though there had never been any evidence of it within their lifetimes. Now it was as though there was a heat in their blood that they couldn't contain. All the wise words in the world could not subdue their desire for action. Perhaps for blood. It should have been enough for them to have slaughtered the cattle. Clearly it wasn't.

'What are you doing here?' Nessa asked them. 'What have you done?'

'What's it to you?' said Conan. He was inevitably in the thick of the trouble; probably the main instigator of it. Nessa had tried to like him for most of her life, but had never succeeded. He seemed to believe that he had got a raw deal from life, though no one could work out why, and was forever on the look-out for anything that he could construe as a personal injustice. He exuded resentment wherever he went.

'That's a really stupid question,' said Nessa. 'You know as well as I do that we're all in trouble if you've gone and messed things up again.'

'Again?' said Conan.

Nessa didn't bother to answer. Conan giggled and one or two of the other cousins joined in. It was Ardy who blurted it out, so bursting with excitement that he couldn't contain himself.

'We took the heads off the cows,' he said. 'We dumped them in their stupid well, didn't we?'

'Oh, no.' Nessa found her imagination leaping forward, through unseen, unimagined steps of escalation, to a state of all-out war. She knew that it always began like this. Small arguments kindled tiny flames. Provocative idiots like Conan and Ardy fanned them into ferocious fires. 'I hope Atticus forgives you,' Nessa went on. 'Because no one else will.'

'Oh, Atticus,' said Conan. 'He's thrilled to bits. Delighted with us. It was his idea in the first place.'

'How do you work that out?' said Nessa.

'He spoke to me,' said Ardy. 'He came to me in a dream.'

When Nessa didn't answer, he sneered and went on, 'Oops. Sorry, O Hallowed One. That's supposed to be your department, isn't it?'

It didn't take the Dogs long to respond. Nessa was still awake when they came through the village at mid-morning. Even if she hadn't been, she would have woken soon enough. No one in the village was able to sleep through the noise and the smell of the fifteen or so young Dogs, most of them on horseback, and their pack of hounds.

Nessa watched them pass from the safety of her little tree house. Their leader was a young Dog she knew well; a butcher by the name of Gowran. Not one of the party, not even the talking hounds who were renowned for their hatred of Cats, showed the slightest hint of aggression. They were even courteous, exchanging polite greetings with the older uncles and aunts. But there could be no doubt in any Cat's mind about their underlying intentions. Their passage through the village was an undisguised display of force. And their return, at dusk the same day, was an undisguised act of terrorism.

They had hunted down and killed two grunts. The carcasses, severely mangled by the hounds, were dragged along behind the horses, their long, matted hair entangled with leaves and bramble vines. The Dogs were as civil as they had been earlier, but there was only one possible interpretation of their actions. The day's sport had been by way of a practice run. If the hounds could kill grunts, they could just as easily kill defenceless Cats.

As soon as they were gone, the villagers held a meeting. It was short and to the point. They were left with no option but to begin to muster arms.

Thursday ~~Saturday~~: February 7

On top of all the work we've already doing in the
garden, Bernard has embarked on a new scheme to
turn the lab complex into a bunker. It was built to
keep the genetic experiments here a secret from any
authorities which might not have approved of them,
and unless you knew it was there you'd never find it.
When the armed gang took over Fourth World, Maggie
and Tina were on their own and they were able to
hide out down there until the men frightened themselves off and went away. It was OK, they said, but
it could have been a lot better. Since there's every
chance the same thing might happen again, we are
going to make proper living quarters down there.

It was snowing hard when we got up, so the garden
was abandoned for the day. Tina has all kinds of
stuff to catch up on with the animals, and Maggie
was ordered by everyone to take a day's rest. Colin
volunteered to have a go at fixing the wheat grinder,
which had been broken for months. He's a bit of a
mechanical whizz kid, that one. He's been tinkering
with engines and things since he was old enough to
turn a screwdriver, and Bernard just leaves a lot of
that kind of stuff to him.

Danny was sleeping all morning as usual, because he
goes fishing during the night, so that left three of us

– Bernard and Sandy and me – to start the work on Project Bunker.

Bernard and Sandy are working hard at rebuilding their damaged relationship. All her life Sandy has lived with a huge chip on her shoulder about her frog genes. She loves her strength and speed and power, but the down-side of having the muscle tissue of a frog is that she looks very strange and has to take care that she doesn't get seen by anyone outside the community, in case it raises suspicions. When she met with the yeti, who also lives in hiding, the two of them developed an instant affinity. So when Bernard told us that he had brought back some of the yeti's hair and intended, against her express wishes, to make a clone of her, Sandy blew a fuse. All her pent-up anger and resentment emerged, and Bernard was forced to confront the effects of messing about with people's genes. It has pretty much blown over now, and most of the time the two of them get on like a bomb. Most of the day it was fun working with them.

We began by moving one of the freezers down there and putting all the fish in it. We froze some carrots as well, and a few rotis – the round, flat bread that Maggie makes on top of the range now that we can't get yeast anymore. We set up a couple of plastic bins for oats but we're a bit behind with the business of porridge production so there's only a few pounds in the bottom of one of them. Another task for the winter evenings. Bernard dug an old electric cooker out of the corner of the garage and, to everyone's amazement, two out of the four rings are working and so is the oven. The plan is to set it up in the room that's now the main lab, but before we do that we have to clear the equipment out and move it into the room that's used as an operating theatre. There's space for all of it in there, so if Bernard and Maggie want to carry on experimenting they can, even though it might be a bit cramped. But the old lab will make a good kitchen/living room. There's already a clean water supply, from a spring they came across when they were digging out the cavity. It's better to drink than the water from the house, which comes down from the little hydroelectric dam. So, in theory at least, we could hole up there for weeks if we had to. Animals and all.

Klaus agrees with me that there's something weird about the yeti's stone. I was on the point of telling Bernard about it today. We were chatting about Tibet and just getting round nice and naturally to the yeti, and I could see my opportunity just around the next bend. But I hadn't reckoned on all that emotional stuff coming back up between Bernard and Sandy. The first mention of the yeti struck a nerve, and the air was suddenly full of awkwardness and tension, and Bernard started whistling and Sandy looked everywhere except at him, so the moment passed and the subject was changed and my chance was lost. It'll come again, I suppose.

2009

Friday ~~Sunday~~: February 8

Loki had her pups! I can't believe it! Tina woke me this morning in a state of high excitement and dragged me downstairs in my T-shirt and raggedy boxers. There they were, six little furry little wrinkly little, blobby little . . . whats? Mongrels. Pi-dogs. Runts. Too small yet, with their blind eyes and snubby noses, to tell who they're going to take after, but a lot of them have their father's yellow colour. Colin says he hopes they don't have his mangy coat and sneaky habits as well, but I said that wasn't fair. He couldn't help the circumstances he lived in, over there in Nepal. In fact, he showed a great talent for survival just by being there at all, when you considered the state of the country at the time. I have high hopes for his children.

Maggie's hopping mad. She says it's not fair that all the others have pipped her to the post. She says she wants to try and devise a way to shorten the human gestation period, but so far she hasn't any ideas how to go about it. As for Loki, I'm not sure whether she shares anyone's enthusiasm, either for her short gestation period or for her offspring. She seems to be totally bewildered by her sudden family and is perpetually muttering about 'basket parasites' and 'belly-limpets' and, for some reason, 'lost property office' and trying to escape from them. Her maternal instincts always win out in the end though, and occasionally she gets caught off-guard and shows how proud she is of them, even though she clearly can't quite figure out where they came from.

Poor Electra's nose is a bit out of joint. Until this morning her kittens were the focus of everyone's attention, and now, suddenly, they're yesterday's news. She wanders in from time to time and makes comments about the puppies which are clearly designed to appear complimentary but have a subtext about the superiority of her own little ones. Tina is bending over backwards to be fair to everyone, but it's still pretty obvious that everyone is besotted with the pups.

I'm the worst. I'm like a proud father because Loki is my dog, and I keep popping in to see them every time I get a moment. The snow is really heavy today so I've been working with Bernard and Sandy again, sorting out all the equipment in the old lab, ready to move it out into the operating theatre. It's amazing how much stuff is down there. I don't understand what most of it is for and I was only half listening when Bernard explained it to me, because I was trying to find excuses to go back to the house. Loki is ravenous the whole time, and I sneaked her an egg at lunch time. Tina bit my head off. We've only got a few hens now and there is only one laying, so all the eggs are being saved for Maggie, because she's eating for two. But Loki is eating for seven, so I didn't feel too bad about it.

Saturday ~~Monday~~: February 9

Bernard says that Loki's brain damage won't have any effect on the pups, provided they learn properly constructed language from the rest of us. I can't wait until they begin to talk.

The snow has started to melt but Bernard wanted to keep going with the lab and negotiated with Maggie to keep me and Sandy for one more day. We packed up most of the stuff yesterday and today we moved it all out into the operating theatre. I still hate going in there. I can never forget the first time I saw the terrible rows of glass jars which hold the mistakes that Bernard and Maggie made along the way in their experiments. I tried hard not to look at them as we worked but it was impossible not to get a glimpse of them occasionally. The feathered baby. The cat with little hands instead of paws. The rabbit with an extra pair of legs. I thought of suggesting to Bernard that we quietly dispose of them, but I was pretty sure what his response would be. As long as the lab was in existence, those horrors would stay there; reminders of the dangers of meddling with nature. Trouble is, it hasn't stopped them. I try not to think about what kind of baby Maggie's going to have. We all know it's another experiment but none of us has the courage to ask the adults what kind of genes it will have and they haven't volunteered to tell us. I'm sure I'm not the only one who has a bad feeling about it. They promised us all that they wouldn't do it any more, but it's like the thing with the yeti hair; it's just another example of Bernard being untrustworthy. Maggie too, this time.

Anyway, we'll know soon enough, I suppose. I just keep praying it won't be ending up in another of those awful jars.

Maybe I shouldn't be writing this down. It has been kept such a close secret for so long, because of what might happen to the animals if anyone ever found out. I'll have to find a good place to hide this diary.

Loki and her pups have moved up to my bedroom, just for a couple of nights, Maggie said, so I can keep an eye on them. I wouldn't put it past Loki to slip away and forget all about them. She has a terrible memory at the best of times. They all start snuffling and whingeing now and again, but that isn't what's keeping me awake now. It's not the jars, either, though the memory of what's in them keeps slipping back into my head. I have to tell someone about the yeti's stone. Every time I put my head down to try and sleep I can sense it there under the mattress. I can't hear it or feel it or smell it. I just sense it. It's almost as though it's alive.

part
two

2009

Sunday ~~Tuesday~~: February 10

Klaus has moved out. I think he doesn't like Loki
and the pups being here. I miss him a bit — I love the
way he sits on the covers with his whiskers twitching
while I write. Oh, well. Perhaps he'll be back.

I spent the daylight hours working in the garden.
Maggie refuses to rest, despite everyone telling her
she has to. She says she's not ill, that pregnancy is
healthy and normal and that there's no reason to
slow down if she doesn't feel like it. But it's clear
that she gets tired. She's bound to. She's as big as
a house. After dark I helped Bernard and Sandy
for a while, but it was obvious from the start that
it wasn't going to be a barrel of laughs. Bernard
was practically plugged into the radio the whole
time, listening to the news, and from Sandy's mood
it seemed he'd been like that all day. There is
more trouble brewing in the Middle East. Even
though most of us never see a drop of oil or anything
derived from it, it's still a big deal with our government. Maggie says they pretend it's about oil but
it's really about religion. Bernard says they pretend
it's about religion but it's really about oil. He says
they have to have oil to keep the army and the air
force going so they can keep fighting with the
Arabs so that they can get oil to keep the army
and the air force going so that (etc.).

We worked away in silence for a while. We were silent, that is. The radio wasn't. Then Sandy suddenly turned it off. Bernard didn't say anything, but his beard fizzed up like a dog's hackles.

'I don't understand why you get so worked up about it,' said Sandy. 'It doesn't affect Fourth World and even if it did, there isn't a single thing we can do about it.'

'It's easy to say that,' said Bernard, doing his best to sound like a benign and responsible parent. 'But we all have a responsibility for the actions of our government. We put them there, after all.'

'And when was the last time we had a general election?' said Sandy.

'That's another issue,' said Bernard, and was about to embark on another treatise about the illegality of the current parliament, who have extended their own term in power indefinitely, when Sandy interrupted him.

'Well, if they ever allow you to vote again you can vote against them,' she said. 'But I won't be able to, even when I'm old enough. And neither will Danny or Colin. Not you, Christie. Nor Tina. As far as the government are concerned we don't even exist.'

That was a new one on me, but when I thought about it, she was right. There would be a record of my existence, and Tina's, somewhere in Ireland, but nothing here. And the others had been kept a close secret since they were born.

Bernard stared at Sandy for a moment, muttered something unintelligible into his bristling beard and turned the radio on again. Sandy winked at me and we all muscled into the work.

The living quarters are pretty much sorted out now, and we have moved on to the bedroom. That's the room where the animals used to be kept while they were waiting for their operations. It was full of cages which had been built into the walls, so there was a lot of unbolting and dismantling to be done. It was tough work because a lot of the bolts were rusted in, but it was great to see the panels coming out, one by one. That room made me uneasy, even when the cages were empty. I suppose we've all changed our opinions of animals, now that most of the ones we know can speak and reason as well as we can.

Loki's worse than ever today. She tried to offload some of the puppies on Electra, and when Electra complained about it and we separated all the little ones out again, Loki got into a seriously confused state and tried to make off with some of the kittens. Oedipus got shirty about it and scratched Loki on the nose. That should have been an end to it. But two of the Dobermen (which is what we call Loki's brothers) were visiting at the time and they had Oedipus backed into a tight corner by the time Tina went in to see what all the commotion was about. I don't suppose any serious damage would have been done, but we rarely have scraps among the animals in Fourth World and it set everyone's nerves on edge.

By dinner time everything seemed calm again. We were all relaxing over the disgusting dandelion coffee that Colin made in the fixed grinder when Electra hopped up on to the table with her tail in the air like a mizzen mast and announced that she had decided on names for her kittens. The two females were to be Cleo and Patra, and the two males were called Bono and Sting. She was so grand in her announcement that we found it hard not to laugh, but we all managed to say suitably flattering things, except for Loki, who skulked around under the table grumbling to herself about 'delusions of grandeur' and 'procurement of asps'.

31

Before I went to bed tonight I spent a while sitting on the floor beside Loki and the pups. I could tell that Loki was still unsettled by the scrap she'd had with Oedipus. She kept rubbing her paw over her nose and knocking off the little round scabs where his claws had dug in. I stroked her dented head.

'Disgruntlepuss,' she said, and stared at the pups as though they were a nest of maggots in an apple she had just bitten into.

'What about names for them?' I asked her. 'Any ideas?' I thought it might help her come to terms with them somehow; see them as individuals rather than just a wriggling hungry mass.

'Freeloaders?' she said.

'No, Loki. I meant names. For each of them, you know?'

I picked up one of the pups at random. He was yellow like his father, but with a broad collar of his mother's glossy black. 'What would you call him?'

Loki gazed at him with a mixture of pride and deep suspicion. 'Greedy?' she said.

'You can't call a dog Greedy.'

'Gutsy?'

'No!'

'Gobbler? Gurgler? Sucky Swagbag?'

'Loki! Come on, now. What about names like the kittens? Think of some famous people.' I picked up another pup, a tiny little one; the runt of the litter. 'This little fellow,' I said. 'What would you call him?'

Loki thought long and hard, a process that was severely taxing for her. I was on the point of calling it a day when the solution burst out of her, like someone realising that they knew the answer to the million-pound question.

'President Globalwarming!'

'Where do you get them from, Loki?'

She looked disconcerted and I quickly changed my tone. 'It's just that it's a bit long, maybe. Bit of a mouthful. Great idea, though.'

But I decided to be prudent and not leave the names entirely to her. She was wildly enthusiastic about every suggestion I made, so it didn't take us long to hit upon names for all six. The three bitches ended up being called Ginger, Cinnamon and Nutmeg, and the dogs were Mustard (Colonel Mustard, said Loki), Pepper (Sergeant Pepper, said Loki) and, despite my gentle efforts to change her mind, President Globalwarming.

Guards were posted at intervals around the village, by day and by night. No young Cat, no matter how experienced he or she might be, was permitted to hunt at night. Instead, well-armed uncles and aunts went out after bigger game – deer and wild goat – which were then shared around the village. Of their own accord, the troublemakers stayed outside the community, living wild in the forest and, doubtless, scheming about trouble to come. No one spoke about what would happen if they decided to return. It was assumed that they wouldn't.

The Dogs made no attack, and as the days went by it became clear that their grunt kill had been a warning to the Cats, and no more. It should have marked the end of the troubles. The villagers were just beginning to breathe easily again when the hot-headed cousins took the law into their own hands and brought disaster upon their own community.

Driven by some corrupted interpretation of heroism, they made a swift, silent raid on the isolated hamlet where Gowran lived with his elderly parents. They murdered Gowran, his three gifted hounds and several of his mute ones. If one of the troublemakers hadn't disapproved of the plan and returned to the village to warn them all, the Cats might have known nothing of it until it was too late. As it was, there was not a great deal they could do, apart from redouble their guard. But there was one vital thing that all the uncles and aunts agreed about. Nessa had to go. She was the one marked with the sign of Atticus; the proof that he had once lived among them and chosen them as his own people. Whatever happened to the rest of them, she had to be kept safe. In the village, among the others, she was an obvious target for retribution. There was only one place that could be considered safe for her to be, and that was the forest. And since a Cat travels faster and lighter alone, and leaves less trace of itself than a group does, there was no question of anyone going with her. Whether or not others should take the young cousins away to the safety of the woods was a secondary question. The priority was Nessa.

She didn't want to go. Whatever her people might have to face, she wanted to share it. But the choice was not hers to make. In this instant she was not an individual with her own rights; she was the common property of the community. They ordered her to leave. They would come for her, they said, as soon as it was safe. A moment later she was climbing the tree-covered hillside beyond the village.

The blackbird was still singing on the branch a few feet from where Nessa was lying. She shifted her position, bringing her legs underneath her, preparing for action. As she gathered herself and made a mental assessment of the branches that surrounded the bird, she quietly reached up to touch her armband and her icon.

I come before you, Atticus, as clean as on the day that I was born.
It was not in my power to bring this bird into this tree to meet its death today.
Atticus designed it so.
Praise him.
It was not my desire that Cats should feed upon the lesser beasts that live upon the earth.
Atticus decreed it.
Praise him.

It is not in my gift to send this blackbird's spirit to a place of
  peace beyond this world, but Atticus can call it there.
As he will call his children's souls
To gather with him in the life beyond.
He will guide our every step.
Praise him.

The prayer, as usual, had the effect of composing her, bringing her into perfect equilibrium and refining her physical judgement. Before uninvited thoughts could intrude and ruffle her mind, Nessa sprang, catching the oblivious bird by one wing before it had a chance to react. With her free hand, she grabbed at a branch to steady herself. The blackbird shrieked in shock and pain and terror. Nessa regained her balance and crouched back down on the rocky shelf that had been her bed. But she got no further with the dispatch of the bird. It stopped flapping and screeching and started pleading.

'Don't eat me! Don't eat me! Gifted bird. I claim immunity under the law! I speak!'

'Oh, no,' said Nessa.

'My wing! My wing! Let me go!'

'I'm sorry,' said Nessa, setting the bird carefully back on to the overreaching branch, where it staggered for a moment or two, unbalanced by the wing that Nessa had grabbed.

'Oh, no,' said Nessa again. The wing was clearly broken. 'Why didn't you warn me?'

'Stupid Cat!' yelled the bird. 'Cats don't eat blackbirds. Cats know we're gifted!'

'Not all of you,' said Nessa. 'I mean, not many of you, even. You were annoying me. I didn't really want to eat you.'

'That makes me feel a lot better, I must say!'

The bird was still off kilter. The wing would neither fold nor straighten, but hung bent and useless to one side.

Nessa reached out. 'Let me have a look.'

'Ow!' shrieked the bird. 'Keep your filthy mitts to yourself, will you? Ow!'

'Filthy?'

'Clean, then. Whatever you say. Keep your lovely clean murderous hands to yourself.'

The bird hopped out of reach, but it was lurching dangerously. If the branch had been the slightest bit narrower it would have fallen out of the tree.

'Listen,' said Nessa. 'Have you got a mate?'

'Yes. No. Yes. I used to have.'

'But you don't have now?'

'As soon as our kids were fledged she went off with some other feathered freak. She didn't talk. There was no reasoning with her.'

'Then you're going to have to let me help you. You'll starve to death up here, and you can't fly down.'

'You won't eat me then?'

'I swear by Atticus that I won't eat you.'

To Nessa's surprise the blackbird gave a squawk of disdain. 'Atticus! You're all as mad as each other, you "civilised" folk. Atticus this, Ogden that. Where did it ever get you except into trouble? And you're at it again now, aren't you? Killing each other?'

Nessa closed a hand round the bird, gently but firmly. He gaped in silent pain and fear.

'What have you seen?'

'Nothing. Nothing. I didn't want to see anything.'

'Others did, though, didn't they? Other birds?'

'Ow! Let me go. I'll tell you!'

'Tell me first.'

'I don't know. There was talk of arrests.'

'Just arrests?'

'Arrests. Imprisonments. And maybe . . . maybe . . .'

'Maybe what?'

'Maybe executions.

'Who? How many?'

'I don't know,' said the blackbird. 'I swear I don't know. But it won't be the end of it, will it?'

Nessa let the bird go. He was right, and she wanted to make sure that she didn't mistakenly take her anger out on him. It wouldn't be the end of it. This was how the wars always began.

Somehow she hadn't believed it could happen. That stuff was all history. It couldn't happen among her village and the neighbours she had known all her life. It wasn't only in the marketplace that the communities interacted. During harvest time on the Dog farms, the Cats would often give up some of their precious sleep to lend a hand, particularly when bad weather was threatening. Afterwards, although it was not customary for the two communities to eat together, tired workers would congregate round the fire and listen to the stories and songs for which the Cats were renowned. There were certain illnesses that only Dog doctors could cure; if and when they arose in the Cat village, there was no problem about calling for help. It had always been freely given.

Not any longer.

Nessa lost all concern for her own safety. If her kinsfolk were suffering, she wanted to share in it, even if it meant disaster for her. This business of being one of the Watchers had always disgusted her. She knew she was different, but she didn't feel different. She had never wanted to be anything other than a cousin, just one of the kids. To their credit, most of her village had always treated her like that. Until now.

Oddly, it was the blackbird who prevented her from returning home and facing the dangers that awaited her there. Where Atticus failed to keep her attached to her own safety, the bird, by virtue of the debt she owed him, succeeded. He was helpless. He depended upon her for his survival. For three days and three nights the bird's needs directed Nessa's actions.

His name, he told her, was Yorick. He was two years old and had fathered two broods of chicks. The second brood had all fledged successfully and taken off to start their own lives. Yorick had no idea where any of them were now. But the first brood had not been so lucky. All four of them had been taken by a pine marten. There had been nothing Yorick or his mate could do. They had screeched and flapped and dive-bombed it, but in the end, one by one, the red devil had murdered their children.

He trembled as he told the story, and Nessa couldn't help feeling a sense of affinity with him. She thought of the small cousins back in the village and prayed that they were safe. They might be. It was possible that this new conflict would never grow to match the savagery that had been unleashed by previous ones. In those, she knew, unthinkable atrocities had been committed by both sides. The young and the old had no more rights than the warriors when bloodlust made people deranged. But Yorick, most of the time at least, kept her mind away from its grisly imaginings. He was clearly in great pain from the fractured wing. However carefully Nessa handled him, she couldn't avoid making the occasional mistake. Despite it all the bird remained even-tempered and stoical. More than that, his own experience of loss made him sensitive to her distress. Nothing was ever said about it, but Nessa was aware that Yorick was nursing her as carefully as she was nursing him.

For those three days, Nessa provided the bird's diet of blackberries and insects. The searching and foraging kept her hands and eyes occupied, even when her mind drifted to more unpleasant realities. Yorick's appetite was good and his instructions about where to find the plumpest grubs were an education to Nessa. The bird lacked nothing in the way of nutrition, but nevertheless it became clear, as time went on, that the wing was not mending. The break was a bad one. It occurred to Nessa that it might never heal.

They took it in turns to sleep, with Yorick on guard during daylight and Nessa during the night. The only hours of wakefulness they shared were the twilight ones, around dusk and dawn. During these they moved through the woodlands, foraging and reconnoitring, searching for the next safe place to rest and sleep. On the first dawn, Nessa returned to the heap of rocks in the hope that, despite what Yorick had told her, the trouble might have died down and someone would have come to fetch her. On the second morning she found that they had wandered too far from the rocks to return in time. By the morning of the third day Nessa arrived at the realisation that, on the pretext of finding good places for gathering food, Yorick had been directing their steps purposefully northwards; in the opposite direction to her village. Her initial panic gradually gave way to resignation. The blackbird was right. The further from the village she went, the better her chances. The conflict would not be resolved in days, or in weeks. If it spread from the original flashpoint, which history told her was all but inevitable, it might take years for any kind of normality to return. She would have to face up to the fact that, for the time being at least, she was alone.

It occurred to her that in time she might come upon another Cat community. Provided it was untouched by the troubles, she was in no doubt that she could seek refuge there. Aside from the armband and icon she bore the mark of Atticus. Among Cats she was more than clan. She was royalty.

In respect of her identity, only one thing troubled her. She had now missed at least one, and probably two, crop days. Her hair had never been so long. There was still not the remotest danger that she would be mistaken for a Dog, even at a distance, but if she remained in isolation for too long it would become a problem. Even if she were inclined to make an approach to civilisation, the only barbers she had ever encountered were Dogs, and she would never, as long as she lived, allow one of them to touch her again, with or without a razor-sharp blade.

She was amazed by the strength of the hatred that had arisen within her since she had heard of the executions. If it hadn't happened, she wouldn't have believed it possible. Dogs had been part of her life for as long as she could remember, but now it seemed to her that she had always hated them; that the mundane transactions between the communities were a sham; acts born out of convenience but which disguised their true sentiments.

All that was over now. It was more than two generations since the last major war between the Cats and the Dogs but everyone knew the stories. Communities would close and become self-sufficient. There would be no trade of any sort until the reprisals and counter-reprisals had exhausted themselves and decimated both populations. Then there would be a lull, lasting years, while the adversaries rebuilt their communities and nursed their spirits back to some measure of health. Only then, slowly and gradually, would communication resume. So it had always been. So it would always be.

Night had recently fallen. Yorick was sleeping, safely perched on a high branch. Beneath him, still high in the tree, Nessa's keen eyes watched the forest floor. She had washed and she had prayed. For the first time since she had taken up with Yorick she was aware of the hunter's keen energy flowing through her blood. It was created by hunger. She had existed for long enough on berries and grubs. She craved meat.

When the hare appeared between the trees she froze; slowed her breathing to a minimum; called upon Atticus.

Patience, to win the friendship of time . . .

If the hare's meandering path brought it beneath her she

would drop like a swooping hawk and the night's work would be a short one. The hare stopped, examined the surroundings with its big ears, bent cautiously to nibble at a bunch of fresh shoots.

Silence, to win the friendship of action . . .

The hare chewed. Listened. Chewed again. It sat up on its hind legs, looked around with its ears again, then ambled away. In the wrong direction.

Nessa was in conflict. She was reluctant to leave Yorick, even for a short time, but she needed meat. Even more than meat, she realised that she needed the intense, all-absorbing thrill of the chase. It would have the effect, she knew, of clearing the polluted pools which had gathered in her mind. For the duration of the hunt, her thinking would run clear and pure.

The hare was already out of sight. Nessa hesitated a moment longer.

Courage, to win the friendship of death . . .
Atticus will guide your steps.
Praise him.

Swiftly and silently, Nessa slipped down from the tree.

The hare, as it turned out, was a wise one. It was dawn before Nessa finally got a grip on it and even then it didn't give up without a fight. Her lip was cut and her jaw bruised by kicks from its powerful hind legs, but the injuries gave her all the more pleasure in her victory.

It wasn't until that feeling subsided that she realised how late it had grown and how far she had travelled. She had been partly right in her thinking when she set out. It was true that the intense concentration throughout the hunt had temporarily eradicated her grief and outrage. But another area of her mind had become dangerously muddied in the meantime. She had covered miles in pursuit of the hare. It would take all her feline instincts for her to find her way back to the tree where she had left Yorick. Worse than that, it was already broad daylight. She would be travelling during Dog time, when her eyes were at their weakest and the likelihood of encountering enemies was at its highest. She considered the possibility of staying where she was; eating the hare and hiding out in a good tree until darkness fell again. But to her amazement she found that her attachment to the blackbird far outweighed her concerns for her own safety. She could not abandon him. She had to go back.

It was raining gently but it wasn't cold. As she began to retrace her steps, a small party of grunts burst from a thicket where they were foraging, swung up into the trees and vanished into the shadows. The sight of them made her uneasy, and not only because of the unpleasantly vivid memories they evoked of Gowran's threatening hunt. Some other thought nagged at the back of her mind, a thought that she had effectively repressed when it first threatened to emerge several years before. She had been out in a far-flung corner of the forest with two of her aunts, gathering a rare fungus that was used in the treatment of chest ailments, when a huge band of grunts had passed beneath the tree where they were sleeping for the day. It was the first and only time Nessa had seen them close at hand. There had been something about them then that sent creeping claws across her skin. She hadn't wanted to think about it then, and she didn't want to think about it now.

It took a good part of the morning for her to get back. She found her way by pure instinct. If she stopped to think about why she was taking one direction and not another, she became confused and disorientated. The instinct only worked if she forgot about it and allowed her mind to dwell on other things. So she thought about her hunger, and the pleasure it would be to satisfy it. She would share the hare with Yorick, offering him the tenderest parts of the innards. Afterwards she would sleep off the deep tiredness caused by the intensity of the night's work.

She was almost at the tree where she had left him when a tension in the forest around her made her stop in her tracks. The birds were silent. Something was wrong. Her hackles rose, even before the dreadful sounds came cutting through the damp air. It was Yorick, his voice shrill and clear, crying out again and again in some terrible agony. The sounds had barely begun to register when another impression reached her heightened senses. A smell. One that there was no mistaking. She had been familiar with it all her life.

It was Dog.

Monday ~~Wednesday~~: February 11

The stone is driving me mad. I kept waking up all through last night, dreaming about it. I was definitely going to tell Bernard about it this afternoon, but when I got down to the lab he wasn't in the mood to hear about anything like that.

He had finished taking out the cages and had scrubbed out the empty room. While he waited for the floor to dry, he was doing a bit of sorting out in the computer room. The radio was on, tuned to Radio Fightback, the pirate station that is operated from an abandoned warehouse somewhere around Edinburgh. It's the only station he or Maggie will listen to. The government channels, according to them, tell nothing but lies.

I could sense his irritation even before I heard what it was that was bugging him. Our government had started dropping bombs on the Middle East again.

I feared for Bernard's blood pressure. In a conciliatory kind of way I started to help with the books he was organising, but since I had no idea what system he was using I wasn't much use.

'Put that pile there outside the door,' he said. 'They're on the way out.'

They were mostly electronics texts, manuals for long-defunct computers and printers and out-dated software languages. I stacked them in the corridor, more carefully than I needed to. When I went back in, Bernard had turned off the radio and lapsed into a more philosophical frame of mind.

'Do you know what I think our worst mistake might have been?' he asked me.

'Being born?' I said.

He laughed. 'Very likely. But since we were, and since we've done what we've done, wouldn't it be terrible if the best we've achieved here turns out to be the worst?'

Pretty much everyone was agreed about what Fourth World's best work was. 'You mean the missing link?' I said.

He nodded. 'The missing link.'

'How could it be bad?'

'I hope it isn't, but I do get the heebie-jeebies about it sometimes. Think about it. What makes the talking animals different from their parents and grandparents who can't talk?'

'The gene,' I said. 'They can think and reason. They have language.'

'And what makes us different from the apes?'

'Same thing, I suppose.'

Bernard nodded again. 'And what have we done with it? This wonderful ability to use reason?'

I knew what he wanted me to say. We had been here before. I didn't oblige him, though. 'We've created music and art and literature,' I said. 'We've developed agriculture and communities. We've learned to store up food every autumn so we don't go hungry during the winter.'

'Well,' said Bernard, 'that's . . . well . . . I suppose all that's true. But . . .'

I finished his 'but' for him. 'We've also developed the most amazingly sophisticated ways of killing each other.'

I'd spent enough time thinking about it. The animal kingdom had savagery in it, but it was an insult to the beasts to claim that human behaviour was bestial. Carnivores killed for food. Other than that, even in the most furious fights over mates or territory, it was almost unheard of for an animal to kill one of its own species. Murder, revenge, punishment, war; they were all human creations. The products, perversely, of intelligence.

'I hope you're wrong, Bernard,' I went on. 'I think you are. I can't see the animals starting to lay landmines and drop cluster bombs on each other. Can you?'

Not even Bernard's grim imagination could see into that bleak future. He smiled and sighed. 'Sorry for being a wet blanket,' he said. 'We can leave these books here. Let's go and see if that floor is dry yet.'

T hree things might have given Nessa good reason to pause had her rage not been racing beyond her control. The first was that Yorick was alive and, apparently unharmed, sitting on a rock beside the tree. The second was that the Dog, whose scent had reached her at the same moment as Yorick's cries, was someone she knew well. The third was that he had a long, sharp knife in his hand. She saw all these things as she flung herself upon the scene, but she registered none of them. Her mind was blighted by fury. She sprang at the Dog with the full force of her headlong run and brought both of them to the ground in a violent tangle of limbs and teeth.

'Nessa! Stop!'

The words reached Nessa's ears but not her consciousness. They might have been swallows flying through the clearing for all the notice she took of them. The Dog was beneath her, scrambling to dislodge her. She was using every weapon she had: teeth, nails, fists, knees. All her blows were hitting home. If only she could find a good, heavy stone . . .

She paused momentarily to look for one. A few rocks protruded among the tree roots, but if there were any loose stones they were hidden beneath the thick build-up of leaf-mould. What Nessa did see, however, was the knife that had fallen from the Dog's hand as he fell.

She made a grab for it, but the Dog took advantage of the momentary respite and, with a strength that surprised Nessa, threw her off him, away from the rocks and the knife. She was on her feet in an instant but so was he, and his foot was on the knife.

'Stop! Nessa!'

This time the words reached her. It was Yorick's voice, filled with fear and urgency.

'Get a grip on yourself!'

Now she took it in. The blackbird was not only unharmed. His broken wing had been ingeniously splinted with a hazel stick and a length of woollen yarn. The one who had done it for him, her adversary, was Farral, the barber's son from the marketplace. He was a barber himself, now. He had cut her hair dozens of times.

But that was in peacetime. Everything was different now.

'Nessa,' he said.

The knife was in his hand and, even though he showed no desire to use it, Nessa knew it would be foolish to try and attack him again. She glanced at Yorick, whose complicity in his own healing seemed to her like a betrayal. He knew what was happening in her village.

As they stood there, stalemated and tense, a small hound pup emerged from behind a tree and advanced upon Nessa, wagging and cringing. She hissed and spat at it viciously. It crept behind Farral's feet.

He tried again. 'Listen, Nessa . . .'

But Nessa was not remotely interested in listening to anything. She wrinkled her nose as though the smell in the air offended her. 'I have to wash,' she said.

2009

Tuesday ~~Thursday~~: February 12

I think the pups might be keeping me awake after all.
They mumble and grumble a lot, and some of Loki's
sighs are way off the Richter scale. Poor thing. She
doesn't know what's hit her. One minute she was a
puppy herself, skitting around the place and getting on
everybody's nerves. Overnight she's a mother, with
these six big gaping gobs going at her round the clock.
I don't envy her one bit – or Maggie either. I'll take
being a boy any day, even if it's not the height of
fashion.

I got as far as telling Bernard about the yeti's
stone. His reaction was a bit disappointing, to be
honest, and I wished I'd told Maggie instead. I suppose
I told him because he was with me in the Himalayas
at the time and she wasn't, and because he's the
one who's mad in to all this research and trying to
find the origin of the missing link. I would have
expected him to be really excited about it, but all
he said was, 'That's interesting. It did cross my mind
to wonder whether they had got around to the business of using tools.'

I suppose that annoyed me a bit. It was as though he
had lost interest in the yeti now that the prospect of
cloning her is gone for ever. Come to think of it, from his
point of view the whole exercise was a bit of a
disaster. Some interesting stuff came out of it in a

way, but it didn't bring Bernard any closer to what he was hoping to find out. We know a lot about the missing link's role in human evolution but we still haven't a clue how it got there in the first place.

Anyway, he might have forgotten about the yeti, but I haven't. An hour doesn't pass that I don't think about her, alone up there in that cold, bleak place with nothing to contemplate but her own death and, with it, the death of her entire race. It's a funny thing, knowing about something like that and being powerless to change it. The sadness of it follows me around wherever I go.

Another round of grumbling from the pups. Another express-train sigh from Loki.

Anyway, I told Bernard that there was something funny about the stone and he said I should bring it down for him to have a look at. I went off to get it but I knew he wasn't really interested, so when Danny asked if I wanted to go down to the shore and help him build his lobster-cages, I agreed.

It's a brilliant idea that he had. We used some of the panels from the animal room. Danny did all the underwater work. I just sat on the rocks and handed him the bits. He built two cages to hold lobsters, so we can have them fresh whenever we want. He says the steel won't last more than a year or two in the sea but it might as well rust usefully as uselessly.

It was nice to be there. I don't see half enough of Danny. He feels much more like a brother to me now than he did when we were living together in Ireland. Being there beside the sea reminded me of The Privateer and made me restless to go travelling again. But not now. Not for a while.

On the way back up the glen I told Danny about

the stone. He was all gung ho about having a look at it, but as soon as we got to my room, he went all gooey about the pups and before we'd finished messing around with them Maggie came thundering along the corridor in a frump because I had forgotten that it was my turn to cook the dinner. We had a bit of a thrown-together meal of fried fish and spuds and broccoli, but no one seemed to mind. I wanted Bernard to ask me where I'd been and why I hadn't brought the stone, but he seemed to have forgotten about it. Instead he started up another of his dinner-time discussions. It began in the usual way, with him making a pronouncement.

'There are two kinds of people in this world,' he said. 'Dog people and cat people.'

His statements were almost always designed to be provocative, and he got a whole heap of responses to that one.

'Rubbish,' said Tina. 'I like dogs and cats just the same.'

'Same here,' said Danny.

'What about frog people?' said Sandy.

'It's true,' said Electra, from her boxful of kittens on top of the sideboard. 'There are dog people and cat people, and everyone in this house is a dog person.'

'That's not true, Electra,' said Maggie, 'and you know it.'

'Aren't there enough arguments in this house already, without you stirring it up?' I said. I didn't normally speak to Bernard like that, but I was still narked with him for not being interested in my stone. 'Even if anybody did like dogs more than cats or cats more than dogs, it isn't going to do anybody any good to start admitting to it, is it?'

'I wouldn't dream of suggesting any such thing,' said

Bernard. 'And you're all leaping to conclusions. I didn't say anything about liking cats better than dogs.'

'You said there were cat people and dog people,' said Sandy.

'And that's what I meant. It's not my idea. It's a well-known hypothesis. There are some people who are like cats; they like to spend a lot of time on their own to pursue their own interests and they can't be bothered with all this hanging around in gangs and being sociable. And there are other people who don't feel right at all unless they're working or having fun in the middle of a crowd.'

'I'm definitely a cat person, then,' said Sandy. 'But I probably wouldn't be if I hadn't been born half frog.'

'You're not half frog,' said Maggie. 'You're nowhere near half frog.'

'I'm a dog person, me,' said Tina. 'I tried the cat life, living on my own. Doesn't suit me one bit.'

'I'm a cat person,' said Colin.

'No you're not,' said Sandy. 'You're more of a dog person than any of us. You follow Bernard around like his shadow.'

'I do not,' said Colin furiously. 'I'm always off doing things on my own.'

'You're never on your own!' said Sandy. 'I'm the one who's always-'

'All right, all right!' Maggie put her hands up like a traffic policeman and called the table to order. 'We should all know better by now than to let Bernard wind us up. Here's what I think. I think we all have a bit of dog nature and a bit of cat nature in us. We're all good at working as a team when we need to, but most of us like to get away on our own from time to time and find a bit of space.'

'Space,' echoed Loki longingly, from the doorway.

'And who says cats want to be off on their own all the time anyway?' said Oedipus, who was curled up in a large cardboard box with Oggy. 'Just because we're independent and don't need to be sucking up to people all the time . . .'

Oggy growled. Electra stood up in her box and hissed. The Dobermen jumped to their feet, hackles raised.

'Now look what you've started,' said Maggie to Bernard.

'I still say there are two kinds of people,' he said.

'There are,' said Maggie. 'There are women, who are the basic, successful model. And then there are men.'

'Oh,' said Bernard. 'Like that, is it?'

The animals returned to their beds. At the table, the people rolled up their sleeves for round two.

When she had washed at the cold little spring, Nessa set out, alone, into the forest. Her sheepskin had come adrift during the fight with Farral and she had left both it and the hard-won hare back at the tree. She would not go back for either of them, or for Yorick. He had a new protector now. He didn't need her any longer. Without her realising it, Atticus had been guiding her steps during the night. She was where she was meant to be. She was moving again as a Cat should move: wild, unencumbered, free.

But Farral, it appeared, was not of the same opinion. She had not gone far from the spring when he caught up with her. 'Don't run away from me, Nessa,' he said. 'We were always friends, you and I.'

It was true. Nessa remembered how she had looked forward each week to crop day and to the gentle manner in which Farral attended to her hair. He invariably took ages to cut it, even though the job was as routine to him as breathing. They needed time to catch up on each other's news, even when neither of them had any. It couldn't be denied that they had been friends. But there could be no more friendship now between Cat and Dog.

'That was then, Farral,' she said. 'This is now.'

'Don't do this, Nessa. I understand what you're going through, but—'

'You don't,' she cut in. 'How could you?'

'All right. I don't. But I can imagine.'

Nessa took a step away from him, accidentally kicking the clumsy pup, who was still doing its best to make friends with her. 'Get this foul creature out of my way before I give it a proper kick!'

Farral flinched. In his society, the talking hounds were regarded as equals. Nessa might have been threatening to kick a small child. Even so, he refused to rise to her challenge. 'Just listen to what I have to say. That's all I'm asking of you.'

Nessa shook her head and tried once again to move away. It was Yorick, speaking from the pocket of Farral's jacket, who succeeded in stopping her.

'He has come a long way to find you, Nessa. The least you can do is hear what he has to say. You might be surprised.'

2009

Wednesday ~~Friday~~: February 13

I knew there was something weird about that stone, but I didn't for one moment expect anything like what happened today. I took it down to the bunker this morning, even though I had been nabbed by Maggie for manure duty. I'd had another sleepless night and I just didn't want the whole thing to drag on any longer. Bernard was in the animal room, measuring up and marking the walls for bunk beds. It's not a big room and he has to fit seven of them in there, so it's taking quite a bit of mathematical juggling. For a moment I thought he wasn't even going to stop and talk to me. When I first unwrapped the stone he just took a quick glance and then turned back to his tape measure. But then he looked again and said, 'Mmm,' then took the pencil out of his mouth and said, 'I see what you mean.'

He took it from me and moved under the light. 'It probably is an axe-head,' he said, 'but it isn't like any kind of stone I've ever seen.'

He weighed it in his palm. 'It's very heavy. Very dense. Seems more like some sort of carbon compound, but it's too heavy and too dense to be coal.' He turned it this way and that. 'No reflective surfaces. No crystalline formations of any kind. Strange.' He handed the stone back to me. 'Shall we take a closer look?'

I was all in favour of the idea until I saw him take a hammer and a chisel from the tool box. 'Oh, no,' I said. 'You can't break it.'

'I won't damage it,' he said. 'I'll just chip off the teeniest scrap so we can put it under the microscope.'

I still didn't like it. The stone isn't easy to describe. Although it's shaped like an axe-head it doesn't have any sharp edges. Everything about it is perfectly smooth and rounded. The surface is immaculate. I couldn't bear to see it blemished. 'You can't,' I said.

'We only need a fragment. You won't even notice it, Christie.'

'I will.'

Characteristically, Bernard turned the tables on me. 'All right then,' he said, dropping the hammer and chisel back into the tool box. 'Whatever you like. I don't suppose it would tell us much of interest anyway.'

He's clever, Bernard. As soon as he said that I had to know. He had me all figured out.

'All right, then,' I said. 'But just a tiny, tiny fragment, OK?'

I brought a clean sheet of paper from the computer room and a couple of slides from the lab. We put the stone on the paper and Bernard fetched his tools again.

'Just a tiny little tap,' he said. 'A couple of grains will do us.'

He put the chisel against the stone but immediately snatched it back again. 'Ooh,' he said.

'What?'

'Little shock. Must have picked up some static under your bed.'

I'd never heard of a stone gathering static, but Bernard knew more about those things than I did. A bit gingerly, he replaced the chisel on the dark surface, raised the hammer and gave it the gentlest of taps.

Neither of us has the faintest idea what happened next. Or at least, we know what, but we don't know how. The moment he delivered the blow with the hammer, Bernard was flung backwards with such force that he slammed into the pile of timber lying behind him. The hammer and chisel flew in opposite directions and clattered off the walls. I jumped up to help Bernard. He was winded and a bit bruised by the hard landing, but otherwise he was OK. It took him a while to get his breath and his voice back, and when he did, his reaction was predictable.

'!?*!!!<<**@??>*!'

We shut the door on the stone and went into the house to tell the others.

No one knows what to do. I never had a problem about touching the stone before, but I'm not mad anxious to handle it now, and nor is anyone else. But we can't leave it there for ever, whatever it is.

I was going to move Loki and the pups downstairs today but I'm a bit on edge and, to be honest, I'm glad to have the company. I thought I'd be able to sleep once I got the business of the stone off my chest, but it hasn't worked out like that. Sleep is further away than ever tonight.

Farral sat on a fallen tree, the hound pup on his lap. It was extremely skinny, Nessa noticed, and trembled persistently. Farral too was considerably thinner than he had been when she last saw him.

'Go on, then,' she said to him. 'Let's hear what it is that you have to say.'

Farral made several poor attempts to get started. 'It's just . . . The way I feel . . . I suppose it's . . .' He had never been particularly articulate, Nessa remembered. What she had liked about him, from the first time he took over the job of cutting her hair from his father, was that he seemed to have a unique outlook on life. He seldom agreed with the accepted wisdom on anything but offered his own interpretations of local events and village life. Sometimes his ideas were quirky, sometimes absurd. Occasionally they were profound and disturbing. He was a rare thing – an original thinker – but he didn't find it easy to marshal those original thoughts into coherent language.

'You see, Nessa . . . It's like this . . .' As he struggled on, Nessa's heart began to warm towards him. It was a feeling she didn't want. She tried to nip it in the bud and steel herself again.

'I haven't got all day.'

Yorick, who was sitting on a branch above their heads, made a series of disapproving ratchety noises, but Nessa's words seemed to have had the desired effect. Farral's mental blocks dissolved and a flood of words flowed out of him.

60

'We're all in this together, don't you see? Injured and injuring, we're all damaged in the same way. We harm ourselves when we harm others. The best in us is atrophied. Defence and aggression turn out to be the same thing.'

'Oh, spare me your puritanical philosophy, Doggy. Don't you realise what's happening?'

'I do, I do. But *you* must realise too, Nessa. There is more than one kind of victim.'

'Is there?'

'I'm on the run too. Just like you.'

Nessa experienced a momentary satisfaction. The Cats must have been making an effort to fight their way out. Perhaps other villages nearby had heard what was happening and come to their assistance.

'Not from your warriors,' said Farral, as though he interpreted her thoughts. 'From my own.'

'Oh?'

'I said no. I said I wouldn't go along with it. I wouldn't kill grunts and I wouldn't have any part in their raids and their mock trials and their executions. I was accused of cowardice and treachery. "You're with us or you're against us," they said. It was a terrible mistake of your people to kill Gowran. He wasn't so bad, you know. He managed to keep some kind of order. People respected him. But the ones who have taken over from him now . . .' He paused. The pup was whining softly. He stroked her ears. 'Anyway,' he went on, 'my choices were simple. Join them or leave. That's why I'm here. We're both refugees now.'

The word was one that, throughout Nessa's life, had belonged to stories of the past, along with the rest of the language of war. In emerging into the present it dragged other words along with it. Tactics. Strategy. Hostage. Reprisal. Torture. More came pushing up behind them, but Nessa avoided them. 'Tell me what happened,' she said.

'What?'

'After I left the village. What happened that you didn't want to be part of?'

Farral seemed unable to answer. Nessa prompted him. 'I know there were executions.'

Still Farral stayed silent.

'If you had no hand in it,' said Nessa, 'why can't you tell me? Go on. I won't bite.'

Farral took a deep breath and spoke, but he couldn't meet her eye. 'They surrounded your village. Gowran's gang. More. Most of my brothers. They demanded that you hand over the people responsible for the murders.'

'Knowing that we couldn't do it,' said Nessa. 'Knowing that Con— that the killers weren't anywhere near the village by then.'

Farral nodded unhappily. 'They knew that all right,' he said. 'I tried to talk sense into them, but there was no point.'

Nessa knew what was coming next. It was a tactic that had been used in the previous troubles, and in many another war back over the ages.

'Until the Cats handed over the guilty ones, our soldiers would—'

'Soldiers already?' Nessa broke in.

'They are calling themselves soldiers,' said Farral. 'They took one hostage from the village every day.'

'And executed them?'

'I didn't have any part in it, you know that. That's why I'm here, not there. We're on the same side.'

Nessa spat. The pup jumped and whimpered.

'We are not on the same side of anything,' Nessa said. 'You're a Dog. I'm a Cat. There is no way that we can ever, ever be on the same side of anything.'

Farral was crestfallen. 'OK,' he said. 'I was wrong, then. I won't bother you any further.'

'Good,' said Nessa. 'I don't know what else you were expecting.'

Farral spoke quietly, but there was a gravity in his voice which gave his words a surprising authority. 'I was expecting you to want what I want. That those deaths in both our villages should be an end and not a beginning. I thought you might understand that vengeance is a disease, not a cure. I thought we might join together and try and find a new way to look at all this.'

'Are you as mad as you sound?' said Nessa. 'What if I did agree with all that? We're two . . . We're two . . .'

'Kids?'

'Not kids. All right – kids. We're two kids. Whatever way we look at it there's nothing we can do.'

Farral sighed deeply. 'I suppose you're right,' he said. 'I suppose I'm just a stupid dreamer. I should have stayed where I was and joined in with my brothers.'

Into the long, long silence that followed Nessa eventually dropped words that had never before passed between a Cat and a Dog.

'I killed a fine big hare last night. Come with me and we'll share it.'

2009

Saturday: February 14
St Valentine's Day

part
three

In the normal course of events Cats ate their meat raw. They reserved the forest fuel to sell to the Dogs, who cooked all their food, and for the occasional ceremonial feast where large game would be roasted and shared. But that day, in deference to her guest, Nessa made no objection when Farral started a small fire and roasted the hare. In the event, all four of them were too hungry to wait until the meat had cooked through. Half raw it tasted fine to all of them and was just about big enough to fill the four stomachs.

Despite her efforts to stay awake, Nessa dozed off beside the dying embers. When she woke, soon after nightfall, she found that Farral had laid her sheepskin over her and was now asleep himself, curled up among the tree roots with the little hound pressed tightly against his chest.

Nessa missed Ossacle, her own special companion from among the gifted crawling cats who lived among the trees in the village. If there had been time, she would certainly have sought her out and brought her along for company. The temptation to return to the village was strong. She glanced at the young Dog and his pup, amazed by what had happened between them. Communal eating was a religious ritual in the Cat community. It happened once a week on Atticus Night and on several other auspicious occasions during the year. The whole village gathered; fires were lit and bread was baked; there were prayers and chants and stories throughout the night. Other than that, apart from the times they might bring a gift to a young cousin or a mate, Cats ate what they caught in the night alone. In sharing her kill with Farral, Nessa had not only engaged in an act of extraordinary intimacy; she had committed sacrilege as well. She tried to remember what it was he had said that had provoked such a strong response in her. Vaguely, she recalled some of his words. More accurately, though, she remembered the spirit behind them. A new thought occurred to her, pure and fresh. It was one she would keep and remind herself of from time to time. Sometimes it took more courage to be peaceful than it did to go to war.

Nessa stood up. She must wash. She would do that before deciding what to do next. Farral's knife was in its sheath at his side. It would be easy for her, with her practised stealth, to slip it out and take it with her. If she decided not to return it would be a useful thing to have. Yesterday she would have done it, but already a new structure was beginning to replace her damaged moral framework. Farral was a Dog but he had not harmed her. She would not harm him.

At the spring, Nessa washed more meticulously than ever, as though she could remove the stains of her unprecedented sins. Afterwards, reborn in cleanliness, she prayed to Atticus.

'I stand before you, father, as clean as on the day I was
  born.
Hear my prayer.
Clear my troubled mind.
Guide my confused steps.'

She waited. She stood on one spot and turned in a slow circle. Only one direction exerted a pull on her, and that was back the way she had come, towards Yorick's tree.

'Hear me, Atticus. Guide me.'

A wild goat and her half-grown kid stepped into Nessa's field of vision. They approached the spring and drank, then browsed on the brambles and willows nearby. When they set out again, following their own narrow paths through the forest, Nessa went after them. Her silent pursuit led her far and wide through the woodland, but when she finally closed in for the kill she discovered that she had company. Farral's pup, woken by the commotion, had come to investigate. The goats had led her in a long, wide arc, through the forest and back again. The kid met its death less than fifty paces from Yorick's tree.

Nessa's sleep was disturbed several times the following day. There was a lot of movement around the camp, accompanied by the soft voices of Farral and Yorick and the excited chatter of the pup who, like a young cousin, could not remember to keep quiet. But the disturbances, incongruously, improved the quality of the sleep she did get. Even though she was far from reconciled to the renewed relationship with Farral, she was comforted by his presence. When she woke fully, an hour or so before dark, she was refreshed and, though she could not see why, optimistic.

Farral had skinned the goat kid and butchered it. A neat pile of sticks was waiting in the previous evening's ashes and a good supply of firewood stood nearby. Yorick was sitting on a fallen branch in the process, as far as Nessa could see, of imparting some kind of education to the hound pup, who was applying intense concentration to her paws, or something in between them. The splint must have given Yorick a great deal of relief. For the first time since his injury, his breast was unruffled and every feather was smooth and shining.

'Evening, Nessa.' Farral appeared from the shadows. 'Are you up long?'

'No.' His appearance had given her a momentary sense of security; of her new clan gathered and complete. But she wasn't ready for him to know that yet, and she resisted asking him where he had been.

He told her anyway. 'I went off looking for a whetstone. To sharpen the knife.' He showed her a rough chunk of grey stone. 'It has to be this kind. I haven't got any scissors, you see. But I thought if I could get the blade sharp enough I could cut your hair.'

As Farral set to work, honing the blade with adept, economical movements, Nessa examined her reactions. The revulsion that she had experienced so recently, arising from the thought of being touched by a Dog, had entirely vanished. Farral was familiar to her. No matter how hard she tried, she couldn't rekindle the hatred for Dogs that had been so all-consuming the day before. At least, she couldn't feel it for him. She wanted her hair cut. He had offered. To decline the offer made no sense at all.

She needed to wash but decided to wait until afterwards. She would have to wash then in any case. Any contact with a Dog, no matter how brief or how necessary, made it incumbent upon the Cat to take a bath.

'You know,' said Farral, testing the blade with his thumb and deciding it was not there yet, 'I was thinking today . . . I mean, I didn't think of it before . . . It's not why I . . .'

Nessa laughed despite her carefully applied reserve. 'Spit it out!'

'It's just . . .' He managed to get going at last but failed to conceal the pleasure the words gave him. 'We make a great team!'

The smile left Nessa's face. 'Team' was a Dog word, like 'pack' and 'herd'. Cats could, and did, choose to co-operate with each other when the need arose, but even then they retained a closely guarded sense of independence. The Dog predilection for crowding together at every opportunity disgusted them.

'It's not why I was looking for you,' Farral was saying. 'I didn't think of it then. But I don't know what I'd have done if we hadn't managed to track you down. I was starving, living off brambles and acorns. I tried to hunt but I just can't. Not on my own. Not like you.'

Nessa accepted the compliment without comment.

'And then . . . This thing . . . I was thinking . . . It's mad, you sleeping all day and me sleeping at night. But then it isn't, is it? It's perfect. Because I can watch you . . . I mean, stand watch while you sleep, me and Bonnie.'

'Bonnie?'

The pup, hearing her name, deserted Yorick and came bounding over. 'What you want?'

Farral didn't answer her, but continued on the same tide of enthusiasm, 'And I can make fire and cook and cut your hair, and in the meantime . . .'

'In what meantime?' said Nessa.

'Meal time?' said Bonnie hopefully.

'In the meantime we can be getting to know each other better.' Farral tested the blade again. 'Ready?'

Nessa hesitated. She didn't like the way Farral's thoughts appeared to be leading him. It was in his nature to want to stick together, but it wasn't in hers. She had to admit that his company was a comfort just now, after all she had been through alone. Whether or not she wanted it to continue was another matter. She certainly didn't want him to make assumptions. The ugly word 'team' was still grating on her nerves.

But she did want her hair cut. She selected a reasonably smooth rock and sat down on it. Farral stood behind her. The knife was far from ideal as a tool for cutting hair, but Nessa was willing to put up with the discomfort. It wasn't only her appearance that bothered her. The fortnight's unaccustomed growth made her head feel heavy and hot.

By the time it was over, Nessa was hungry and itching for a bath, but Farral had a request to make of her that drove all other thoughts from her mind.

'Will you cut mine now?'

'What?'

'I've thought about it, Nessa. Ever since I decided not to take sides. I want it to be a gesture.'

'A gesture of what?'

Farral tugged at the thong that tied his thick, brown hair back from his face. 'Our hair defines us, doesn't it? It's one of the things that marks us out from each other. When you see someone, straight away you know who they are. What they are. Which side they're on.'

'But you can't become a Cat, Farral. It doesn't matter what length your hair is. You'll always be a Dog.'

'Maybe. And I didn't say I wanted to become a Cat. I don't want to be either. I want to be something else. I want to walk between the battle lines and find another way.' Carefully, he put the knife into her hand.

'You're mad, Farral,' she said. 'What will happen if they find you?'

'Do it, Nessa.'

She put her hand beneath the heavy bulk of his hair and lifted it away from his neck. 'I can't. I don't even know how.'

He was trembling. 'You'll learn,' he said.

2009

Monday: February 16

Nessa stripped the last of the meat from the bone and tossed it to Bonnie.

'Nothing on it!' the pup complained.

Farral cut a pair of ribs from the roast and gave them to her. She had already wolfed down a good share of the meat from his own part of the kid, but she was growing, or trying to. Her appetite was bigger than she was.

Nessa watched Farral as he wiped his greasy hands on a fistful of damp leaves and picked up a stick to poke at the fire. She had hardly been able to keep her eyes off him all night. The haircut she had given him was extremely rough; as a trainee barber she was a dead loss. But the transformation was astonishing. He would never be mistaken for a Cat, even if he discarded the hound's-tooth torque he wore at his throat. The tattoos on his arms and feet, designed to imitate the hair of a hound, would be there for as long as he lived. But what amazed Nessa was how his face had changed. She had always assumed that there were fundamental differences in the features of Cats and Dogs. Now, she realised that there were not. If she met him now, for the first time, and couldn't see his arms or his feet or his torque, she could easily take him for a Cat. A distant one, perhaps, but a cousin.

Since the haircut he had been in a state of high excitement, as though the removal of the extra weight had liberated him. His eyes were bright and his movements were brisk and purposeful. 'You won't need to hunt tonight,' he said, nodding towards the remains of the kid, which were hanging from the tree. 'There's enough on this for tomorrow.'

'What would I do if I didn't hunt?' said Nessa.

Farral shrugged. 'Rest?'

'I've done that already.' There was no way to explain to him what hunting meant to a Cat, but Nessa tried to anyway. 'It's not just about getting food. It's as much about the forest and the night. It's what we are. When I'm out there in the dark I become part of it. I use every instinct I was born with and a lot that I've learned. When I'm hunting, I'm . . .' She struggled for the right words. 'I'm completely alive. I'm authentic.'

A light drizzle was falling and the fire was smoking badly. It made Nessa profoundly uneasy, but the stupidity of what they were doing continued to elude her. She had fallen into a false sense of security, assuming that, since the enemies she feared were Dogs, then all Dog ways must be safe.

Farral pulled the unburned sticks to the edge of the fire and began to heap leaf-mould onto the embers to quench them. 'Authentic is a great word,' he said. 'That's how I feel now. Doing what's right for me. What I've always wanted to do.'

'You mean cutting your hair?'

He grinned and ran his hand, for the hundredth time, through his scraggy locks. 'No. Even before this . . . conflict . . . I've always wanted to make some kind of stronger link with your folk. Try and understand what divides us. What the root causes were.'

'Root causes?'

'I suppose they're buried too far back in the past. But there might be ways of trying to dig them out.'

'What kind of ways?'

Farral glanced at her and she could see that he was apprehensive. 'We could exchange our stories.'

It was a step too far. There were Cats in Nessa's community, and in others, who were famous for the stories they told. There were Dogs who would creep to the edges of the circle during the Cat festival nights in the hope of hearing a new work by one of the more renowned storymakers, and others who would pay them handsomely to come to a Dog party and entertain the guests. But Farral wasn't talking about that kind of story. What he was proposing was far more disturbing than that.

It made Nessa aware that she was forgetting herself. She had slept, she had borne the touch of a Dog and returned it and she had eaten, all without washing. She needed to be more careful if she wasn't to be led into very grave danger.

2009

Tuesday: February 17

Taking the pheasant was almost too easy, like picking an apple from a tree. For that reason they were scarce in the woods round Nessa's village, and this one would be a special treat. The question of whether she would eat it alone or with the others occupied her for most of the rest of the night.

She padded through the forest, deep in thought. What Farral had said about the stories had shaken her deeply. It was a profane idea. The name of Atticus was never uttered within earshot of a Dog, even though it was known to every one of them. The legends that surrounded him, which formed the basis of the Cat religion, were closely guarded, as were the Dog stories about their own false idol, Ogden. The idea of sharing these closely guarded secrets with Farral made Nessa's skin crawl.

She had, she realised, been taken in by him. The concept of spies was familiar to her, but she had always considered it a far-fetched idea; as far-fetched as the belief that fuse lidges – the heaps of rust that lay in the plains beyond the Dog village – had once flown through the air. But perhaps there really was such a thing as a spy. What if Farral had been sent out to find her? Not to kill her, perhaps, but to corrupt her; to undermine one of the Watchers, who were so important to her people. To alienate her from the one thing that could sustain her in her isolation. To separate her from her culture and her identity.

She shuddered. At a small stream which ran down a steep embankment she washed meticulously and prayed fervently:

'No Cat need ever fear to walk alone . . .'

Atticus inspired her with righteous anger. She had been polluted but she was clean again now. She would not entertain any further attempts to undermine her. But she would, she decided, return to the camp. She would string Farral along for one more day and then she would leave. This time, though, she would take Yorick with her.

2009

Wednesday: February 18

The pheasant, jointed and grilled over the flames of a fresh fire, made a wonderful breakfast for Farral and a bedtime snack for Nessa. This time the sharing grated on Nessa's nerves but she tried not to let it show. For his part, Farral was bubbling over with gratitude and enthusiasm.

'Could you teach me, do you think? I can already see in the dark. Not as well as you, obviously. I can imagine it, though . . . What you were saying . . . about being part of the darkness.'

Nessa smiled and nodded, resisting giving expression to the derision she was feeling. The idea of a Dog bumbling about in the forest and pretending to be a Cat was one of the most absurd images that had ever occurred to her. Apart from anything else, the entire forest population would smell him a mile off.

He babbled on: 'And I could teach you how to work as part of a team. Me and you and Bonnie.'

This time Nessa could not hold her tongue. 'If we needed to hunt in packs, don't you think we'd have worked it out for ourselves?'

'Sorry,' said Farral.

'It's all right.' Nessa stood up and stretched. A bath, a prayer and a sleep would set her up to put a good distance between them the following night.

'I didn't mean to offend you,' said Farral. 'It's just part of the way I'm thinking. To get to know each other better.

Completely. Understanding is the first step towards forgiving and forget—'

He stopped, cut short by a low growl from the pup. Two trees away a fox was sitting, observing them.

'Ho, brother,' Farral called to it. 'Are you gifted?'

The fox remained where he was for a long moment, then stood up and, extremely cautiously, began to approach the camp fire. At a safe distance he sat down again, one ear trained on Bonnie, the other on Farral. 'It's a bad dream,' he said. 'Two Cats with a hound pup.'

Farral held up a tattooed arm and rattled his torque.

'Worse again,' said the fox. 'You show every sign of being out of your minds, both of you. If you weren't you wouldn't be sitting here like broody ducks waiting to be scrunched alive.'

'Scrunched alive?' said Nessa. 'By who?'

'Word travels slowly to the deaf and the stupid,' said the fox. 'Where have you been? You must be the only creatures in the forest who don't know what's happening.'

'Tell us, then,' said Farral.

'The place is overrun with Dogs,' said the fox. 'Dogs on horseback and their slobbery hound-packs. Looking for you lot –' he glanced pointedly at Nessa – 'but I wouldn't be surprised if they were quite happy to get their teeth into you as well, Dog.'

'What do you mean, looking for my lot?' said Nessa.

'They attacked the guards. Bloody business. Broke out of the village and scattered through the woods. The Dogs got some of them straight away, of course. It isn't easy to travel fast with young ones in tow. Some of them are still on the run, though. The Dogs are widening the net. Not far behind me now.'

Simultaneously, Nessa and Farral moved their lips in silent prayers to their respective gods.

'I could smell your filthy smoke a mile off,' the fox went on. 'I wouldn't be too keen to hang about if I were you.'

Nessa and Farral acted in unison, scooping up the sodden mould and pressing it down on to the fire.

'Bit late for that now,' said the fox, his voice betraying a sadistic pleasure in their terror. 'If I were you I'd just leave it and leg it as hard as you can.'

Farral yanked at the remaining joints of the kid, snapping the yarn on which they were suspended. Nessa grabbed her sheepskin and picked Yorick out of the tree.

'Leave me! Leave me!' he squawked.

'No.' Farral took him from Nessa and, already running, slid him into the breast pocket of his woollen jacket. Nessa hesitated, heaping more leaf-mould over a couple of smoky leaks. She was still thinking. If she was serious about parting from Farral, now was the time to do it. Before he even realised that she wasn't following she would be far away, running in a different direction. She almost did it. She would have, if Bonnie hadn't tipped the balance.

The pup was paralysed, torn between her old loyalty and her new one. 'Run, Nessa!' she yelped. 'Come on!'

There was no more time for thought. Together with Bonnie, she lit off after Farral. He was waiting close by, in a patch of mottled sunlight. As Nessa ran past he fell in at her heels.

Before long the initial panic burned itself out of their blood and they dropped their speed to a steadier, more sustainable pace. As her ability to think returned, Nessa realised that, rightly or wrongly, she had made her choice. Wherever it was that their flight might lead them, she and Farral were going there together.

part four

2009

It's almost impossible to write down what has been happening here. I don't even know who I'm writing this for. No one would ever believe it. Perhaps it's just for myself. But in any event I have to write it down, I have to record it.

I can't remember what day it all started. The day after Bernard got knocked flat by the stone, anyway. We spent ages over breakfast trying to work out what to do. In the end we came to the conclusion that it was probably only the presence of metal that had caused the stone to give off that powerful charge, and we decided to move it the way it had been moved before, all the way from Tibet. So Bernard went down to the lab and I went upstairs to get a pair of gloves and the silk scarf that the stone had been wrapped in, which was in the pocket of my other jeans. By the time I got down to the lab complex, Bernard had already been there for a few minutes. I saw him as I walked down the steps. He was standing in the corridor, staring into the computer room. Oggy was beside him, staring in as well. The hackles were up all along his back, which alerted me to the fact that there was something wrong, but he wasn't making a sound. Neither of them paid me any attention.

'Everything all right?' I asked.

They didn't answer. It was as if they hadn't even heard me. I stood beside them and looked into the room, and from that moment on, if anyone had come down the stairs and spoken to me, I wouldn't have noticed them, either.

There was something in there.

A hundred thoughts crashed into each other inside my head: Run! Get the police! Get the army! Get out of here! Get Maggie! Don't get Maggie! Wake up, for God's sake! What I did, though, was exactly what Bernard and Oggy were doing. I stood glued to the floor and stared.

There are two things I can safely say about the thing I saw in the computer room. It was roughly the same height as Bernard. It was brown. After that, we're into the realms of the ludicrous. I can't help that. I'm describing what I've seen. That's all I can do.

He, she or it is alive, I'm pretty sure. Alive as in an independent, organic being, as opposed to a robot or a plant. Beyond that I can only describe the method in which it functions. How it does what it does is beyond my comprehension. I have no idea what, if any, scientific principles it is governed by.

When I first saw it, it had no legs, but it had several snake-like arms, or feelers, emerging from the upper regions of an otherwise formless bulk. It was using these spindly limbs to examine the computer. Some of them ended in various numbers of thin, delicate digits. Others sort of expanded into spongy appendages, with which it dabbed at different parts of the computer. What I soon came to realise was that these attributes were not fixed. Bernard and I had fingers and toes. They were fingers and toes when we went to bed in the evening and they were fingers and toes when we woke up in the morning. As far as we were able to ascertain, they were fingers and toes while we slept as well, whatever our dreams might tell us. Oggy had paws, which behaved in a similar manner. But this visitor – this thing that was taking a close look at our computer – could have whatever it wanted at the end of its arms. I noticed this when it was investigating the mouse. It touched it first with a dozen tiny, ultra-flexible fingers, which lengthened and shortened as they probed it, and even squeezed down into the narrow space between the click buttons. A few seconds later the whole hand flattened out, became paper-thin, and completely enveloped the mouse. It didn't lift it up but it must have felt underneath it and discovered the roller-ball because the edges of the 'hand' retracted until it fitted snugly over the mouse, and then it began to push it backwards and forwards across the mat. Nothing happened, of course, because the computer wasn't on, but that didn't bother the visitor at all. The next thing it did was to change its 'hand' again, producing two stubby digits which it used to press the buttons. Those soft little clicks were the first sounds I'd heard since I arrived in the doorway.

Bernard cleared his throat. It was an anxious, humble sound, quite out of character. The thing made no response. It was probing the underneath of the keyboard and the back of the computer with several arms at once.

'Excuse me,' said Bernard.

Still nothing. One of the limbs had sprouted fifty or sixty long fingers, with which it was pressing all the keys on the keyboard with the speed of a manic journalist chasing a deadline that has already passed.

'Hello?' said Bernard, quite confidently this time.

The thing gave no sign of having heard. As we watched, it demonstrated that not only the appendages but the limbs themselves were impermanent. It retracted several of them at once, assimilating them seamlessly into its brown bulk and then extended, or perhaps grew, another, thicker one, which it plastered against the monitor like a wet towel.

'Christie, listen,' said Bernard. 'Get ready to run, all right?'

'No, Bernard,' I said. 'Leave it alone, will you?'

Oggy growled nervously.

'I'm not going to do anything stupid,' said Bernard. 'I just want to see if I can communicate with it.'

'No!' I was revisited by the frightening image of him being hurled backwards through the air the previous day. Oggy was growling again, a high-pitched, anxious sound.

'Hush, Oggy,' said Bernard. He took a step forward into the room.

The 'thing' opened an eye in its back.

2009

Wednesday ~~Friday~~: February 20

I'm not writing this in my room any more, by the way.
I'm in the bunker, sitting at the bottom of the steps.
It's my turn to be on watch. The visitor has locked
itself into the lab and has been there for nearly two
days. We don't know what it's doing in there and it
won't let us in to find out. So we're taking it in turns
to wait until it's finished whatever it's doing in there.
That should give me plenty of time to write and try
and catch up with this diary, because there's flip all
else to do down here.

I'd got as far as when it opened an eye on its back.
Strictly speaking, neither of those words is right. It
didn't open an eye because the eye wasn't there to
open in the first place. In the same way that it
produces limbs and digits, it produces eyes, at the
time and place they're required. Except that they
aren't exactly eyes, or not what I would think of as
eyes. They're more along the lines of an opaque kind
of lens with nothing in the way of an iris or a pupil.
And as for where it was that the eye opened, it
wasn't much longer before we realised that the thing
doesn't really have a back, or a front for that
matter, or sides or a top or a bottom. Its mass seems
to be entirely malleable; almost fluid. If there is
anything about it that is fixed or permanent, like a
brain or a digestive system, it's out of sight.

Anyway, to all intents and purposes it opened an eye in its back. It looked at Bernard. Of that much I am certain. Bernard froze. He held his breath. We all did.

Nothing happened. After a while the lens disappeared again. There was a click from the computer as the 'thing' discovered how to open the CD-ROM drive. It flattened out the end of an arm and felt around inside it.

Bernard took another step forward. Another lens opened. Bernard hesitated, but this time he didn't stop. The lens followed him, sliding around the thing's body. He continued to edge forward until he was standing beside the bookshelf, just a few feet away from the computer desk. I was terrified, and Oggy was trembling like a leaf. But as soon as Bernard had stopped moving the lens vanished again. It was as though the thing hadn't the remotest interest in anything other than the computer.

'Hello,' Bernard waited a moment, then tried again. 'Are you . . . um . . .'

At that moment the thing discovered the on/off button at the back of the computer and pressed it.

'Oh,' said Bernard. 'Well done. You turned it on.'

He took a step towards the thing, but its entire attention was focused on the computer, which was booting up with all kinds of satisfying wheezes and whirrs. It didn't even afford Bernard the courtesy of looking at him.

Bernard glanced at me and I noticed the old familiar glint in his eye. He was no longer afraid. 'Do you come here often?' he said to the thing.

I suppose it was the relief; the release of all that high tension. I burst out laughing and so did Bernard. The whole situation was suddenly too ridiculous for words. When we finally got our breath back, Bernard said, 'Go and get Maggie, will you?'

I started to go.

'Wait a minute,' said Bernard. 'Warn her first, all right? I don't want her to get too much of a fright. Tell her what it is.'

'OK,' I said. But at the bottom of the steps I turned and went back to the doorway.

'What is it?' I said.

Over the nights and days that followed, Nessa and Farral travelled rapidly north, through the dense belts of forest that spread across the land. They followed no set plan; their rhythm of activity was set by their available energy and not by any pattern laid down by either one's nocturnal or diurnal habits. They moved by the light of day and by the dark of night, running and walking until they were at the end of their strength, then snatching a few hours of sleep whenever they could.

The first days were the worst. It was as well that they had brought Yorick along with them. As well as blackbirds, there were gifted birds among the starling, thrush, magpie, finch and robin populations, but their numbers were relatively low. Without Yorick's special calls and without his affinity with the other gifted birds, they would never have been able to enlist their help. Birds, like most of the other talking animals, were uneasy around Cats and Dogs. Wherever possible they avoided getting drawn into their affairs.

But Yorick soon got the network operating in their favour. Through the contacts he made he learned of the movements of their pursuers. Without that vital knowledge it was unlikely that they would have escaped.

According to the birds, the hunters picked up their trail within a couple of hours of them abandoning the camp fire and followed it until nightfall. There was a long discussion then, about the merits of continuing while the trail was fresh, but in the end it was the fear of guerrilla attacks by the displaced Cats that persuaded the party to stay where they were.

Nessa and Farral heard the news at dawn. They had a good start on their pursuers, and were confident enough that they could stay ahead of them if they continued to move as fast as they could. What they hadn't considered, however, was that the hunters would split up. A pack of hounds, led by several gifted ones, set out to make a wide sweep around to the east, in an attempt to get out ahead and cut off their quarry. If the birds hadn't warned Nessa and Farral they would have run straight into the trap. As it was, they made a rapid change of direction, turning to their west and tracking across a stretch of open moorland into another area of thick forest beyond. They kept moving throughout the day and the next night, even though they were so exhausted they could barely move. But the plan had worked. The following morning the bird network informed them that their pursuers had turned back. There were more fish to fry, after all.

Even so, the sleep they managed to catch that day was shallow and disturbed. They were up well before dusk and moving again. Neither of them needed to say what they both knew. They would not feel safe until they had put a lot more distance between themselves and the ruined communities they had left behind. Worse than that: each of them, in the privacy of their own thoughts, suspected that feeling safe was a luxury that they might well have lost for ever.

2009

When Maggie and I arrived in the bunker I walked
straight over to Bernard, hoping that I looked braver
than I felt. The visitor watched me with its sliding
eye. I had the distinct impression that I was playing a
part in some kind of absurd TV show. Your mind can
play the weirdest tricks when you are faced with
something that doesn't fit with your established sense
of reality. I kept expecting some solution to what I was
seeing, like you do in dreams when the unbelievable
suddenly becomes completely obvious. It was a holo-
gram that had fallen out of the computer, or some
friend of Danny's that had crawled out of the sea. 'I
told you about that thing, stupid.' 'Oh, right. Of course
you did.' It was taking its time to happen, though.

'Anything new?' I said to Bernard.

'Just the wallpaper,' he said.

Maggie was following what turned out to be the
normal procedure: standing at the door with her
mouth hanging open. I had given her due warning, but
this was one of those events that nothing can really
prepare you for.

'There's a thing down in the lab,' I had told her.
'You won't believe it when you see it.'

'What kind of a thing?' she asked.

'I don't know. It's a queer kind of a yoke.'

Where I was born a 'yoke' is another way of saying a

'thing', or a 'thingamajig' or a 'whatsit'. But Maggie had never heard the expression before.

'A yoke?'

'A brown yoke with millions of arms.'

As we walked across the yard to the garage, where the trapdoor is that leads into the bunker, she quizzed me. 'An insect?'

'No. Way bigger. Huge.'

'An animal?'

'I wouldn't say so.'

'What, then?'

'I don't know what it is.'

'But it's a yoke, right?' she said.

The Yoke, as we called it from then on, appeared to be intrigued by wallpaper – the background graphics behind the icons on the computer. When Maggie and I arrived it was trying them all out, one after another, examining each one minutely with a lens that grew out of its middle like a lopped-off branch. It took quite a while to go through them all, and by the time it got to the end of them Maggie had passed through Stage One – the Gormless Gawp – and had come over to join Bernard and me at closer range.

'Are you sure it's not dangerous?' she said quietly.

'Doesn't seem to be interested in us at all,' said Bernard.

'Does it speak?'

'I don't know. It didn't speak to me, anyway.'

'Maybe it doesn't understand English?' I said.

'Could be,' said Bernard. 'What do you suggest? Portuguese? Telugu?'

We stared at it again. There was nothing else to do.

'Should I tell the others?' I asked.

'No,' said Bernard. 'Not yet. There are more than enough of us in here as it is.'

The Yoke clicked on an icon and opened the word-processing programme. The eye came out again and examined the flip-down menus, one by one. It clicked on 'New Document' again and again, until there were about fifteen of them open, each one as blank as the other.

'I don't think it has the remotest idea what it's doing,' said Maggie.

It clicked on 'Open Document' and the window with the file lists came up in the centre of the screen. For ages it clicked with the arrow outside the window. The computer pinged away in useless protest.

'Shall I show it?' said Bernard.

'No,' said Maggie. 'Leave it.'

'I don't think it's going to hurt us,' said Bernard. He took another step and another, until he was standing right beside the Yoke. He pointed to the mouse, all but hidden beneath the mouse-adapted 'hand'. 'Shall I show you?'

The eye watched. Bernard reached out towards the mouse. It was a gesture, really, a crude attempt at body language. He had no intention of touching the Yoke or trying to take the mouse away from it. But the Yoke, it seemed, had no appreciation for such subtleties. From the 'arm', a tiny, hair-like extension shot out and flicked Bernard on the wrist. He cannoned backwards in a sinister repeat of his trajectory of the previous day, collided with Maggie and me and brought us all to the ground in a bruised heap.

We scrambled up and made an extremely hasty exit. Maggie was the primary focus of our concern, but she appeared to be OK.

'Oh, cripes,' said Bernard, as we composed ourselves

in the hallway. 'What on earth are we dealing with here?'

'God only knows,' I said.

'I doubt it,' said Maggie. She rarely lost her temper, but the episode had clearly shaken her badly. She embarked on a furious tirade against Bernard and his total stupidity for exposing us all so recklessly to something he knew nothing about. We might all have been killed, she said.

Bernard took it in his stride, accepting it for the understandable reaction that it was. 'At least I used myself as the guinea pig,' he said. 'I wish I knew what was going on. That's twice in two days. The exact same thing. The same kind of voltage, too. Where is that stone, anyway?'

The door to the animal room, which we had care-fully closed behind us when we left the previous day, now stood open. The hammer and the chisel and the paper were all on the floor, exactly as we had left them. But the yeti's stone was gone.

'You could go back, you know,' said Farral.

It was pouring rain. They were picking blackberries along the scrubby foot of a rock face. Behind them a strong, swift stream roared past. The rock, and the stream bed, contained a large amount of slate in various shades of purple and pink and blue.

'I don't mean back to your village. But any Cat community would take you in. There's no reason for you to stay out here on the run.'

The berries were soggy and tasteless, very different from their sweet, plump relations in the lowlands. These ones were the products of the harsher mountain climate, where rain-laden westerly winds blew in from the sea and the air was constantly damp.

'Are you trying to get rid of me?' said Nessa.

'You know I'm not.'

He was right. She knew that. What she didn't know, and couldn't work out, was why she didn't have any inclination to do as he suggested. It wasn't that the thought hadn't occurred to her. A day seldom passed when she didn't spend time imagining the relative comfort and safety that she could have, in exchange for this perpetual movement through the cold and the damp. She often found that she became irritated with Farral; not because of anything in particular that he did, but because she was not accustomed to spending so much time in the company of another individual. Cats didn't do that. Even within their own communities they tended to keep themselves to themselves for much of the time. Only the very young and the very old had 'best friends' and even then, those relationships were fluid and impermanent. Besides that, she was still not entirely sure she trusted Farral. But she still had no inclination to leave him.

Yorick was hopping about beneath the undergrowth, feasting on insects and thin red worms. His wing was healing rapidly. The splint had fallen off a few days before and Farral had seen no reason to replace it. Yorick was exercising the wing carefully in the safety of the trees but hadn't yet risked flying with it. 'I think she's getting sweet on you,' he said to Farral.

'She certainly isn't,' said Nessa. 'That's a disgusting thing to say.'

'He isn't that bad,' said Bonnie.

'He's a Dog,' said Nessa. 'I'm a Cat. Could you see yourself falling for a fox?'

'If he was gifted, perhaps,' said Bonnie.

'Yeah, sure,' said Farral.

They rounded a bend in the rock wall and surprised a party of grunts, engaged in the same pursuit as themselves, browsing along in the opposite direction. When they saw Nessa and Farral they stopped what they were doing and stared, the mothers clutching their wide-eyed infants.

Bonnie growled.

Nessa watched the grunts as they grouped together, uncertain of how to react. Their bodies were brown and muscular, and their broad shoulders and thick necks gave the impression that they were much more powerful than either Dogs or Cats.

And yet they were otherwise so similar.

Abruptly, Bonnie charged at them and sent them scattering in confusion along the bank of the stream and across it, into the cover of the trees beyond.

'Bonnie!' yelled Farral. She returned to him, her hackles raised. 'There was no need for that,' he said.

'Sorry,' said Bonnie.

But Nessa wasn't sorry. Out of sight was out of mind. She dismissed the grunts and the uncomfortable thoughts that always accompanied sightings of them. 'You could do the same thing,' she said to Farral.

'Do what?'

'Go to a Dog village. Ask for refuge.'

'With my hair like this?'

'Why not? Say you got captured by a bunch of rebel Cats. Say they hacked off your hair.'

'Hmm,' said Farral. 'It might work, I suppose.'

He returned to picking berries and Nessa joined him. Each of them knew that they were not prepared, not yet, to go back to their own people. Nor were they ready, either of them, to talk about why.

2009

Friday ~~Sunday~~: February 22

All of us at Fourth World have seen strange things in our time. Some of us have met the yeti face to face, and we all saw the dead merchild that Danny tried to save when her people were contaminated by a radioactive wreck. There are even those among us who are, themselves, strange things. But none of us has ever imagined, much less seen, anything as strange as the Yoke.

We haven't the faintest idea what to think, let alone what to do. Apart from the four of us down in the lab that morning no one had seen it. Back in the house, later that day, we discussed it. The trapdoor was locked and Hushy the thrush was on watch in the ash tree in the garden, from where he could see both garage doors. We had done our best to describe the Yoke to the others but it was an impossible task. They were curious and excited and baffled but they were also a bit doubtful, as though the possibility existed that the four of us had experienced some kind of mass hallucination.

'Could we get a net over it?' said Colin. 'Or a big blanket or something?'

'Possible,' said Bernard, 'but I wouldn't like to try. I don't know how far it can reach with those tentacles but I do know it's pretty quick off the mark.'

'If we crept up on it, maybe?' said Oedipus.

'No,' I said. 'It doesn't seem to respond to sound but it can sense movement somehow.'

'Maybe there's something it doesn't like,' said Tina. 'Water or fire or something like that.'

'Loki approach,' said Loki.

Everyone answered together, practically in unison. 'What?'

'Loki operation.'

There was a momentary silence while seven human and about ten animal brains tried to make sense of what she had said. As usually happened, they all failed, and the conversation continued without her.

'We could just starve it out,' said Sandy. 'I mean, presumably it needs to eat?'

'It probably does,' said Danny. 'Trouble is, we've just put a freezer down there and provided it with enough rations to last it for weeks.'

'We could just take all the stuff out again,' said Colin.

'Oh yeah?' said Tina. 'You can try it if you want. I wouldn't like to be the one caught raiding its larder.'

'What about trying to get outside help?' I asked. 'The police? The army?'

I was the only one in the whole community who held to the idea that there was a benign state some-where out there beyond the boundaries of Fourth World that represented order and normality. Even as I made the suggestion I realised that it was a figment of my imagination or, at best, a memory from the dead and buried past. The rest of the Fourth World residents, without exception, had spent most, if not all of their existence in hiding from the authorities. They had never experienced the reassuring faith that I had once held in the great 'Them' who existed to protect their citizens and their way of life.

My contribution met with exactly the same blank kind of response as Loki's.

'I think we should just shoot the flaming thing,' said Tina.

'Great idea,' said Colin. 'Except we haven't got a gun.'

I thought I detected a smug expression on Tina's face, but my attention was drawn elsewhere before I could think about it. Loki was bumbling around under the table anxiously. 'Loki,' she said. 'Lokee!'

'Cut it out, will you?' I said to her. 'You're getting on everyone's nerves!'

'I don't believe the way you lot are talking,' said Maggie. She hadn't spoken before. It was a recurrent tactic. Her words, as they usually did, carried all the more weight for being few and far between. 'We're in the amazing position of being visited by the most extraordinary creature any of us has ever seen and all you can do is try and think of ways to get rid of it. I could understand that if it was a threat to us, but I haven't seen any sign that the Yoke means us any harm.'

'No harm!' spat Bernard.

'I know you got zapped,' said Maggie, 'and I don't want to suggest that it wasn't a pretty nasty experience. But it seems to me that the Yoke was only acting in self-defence.'

'I didn't even touch it!' said Bernard.

'I know you didn't, but as far as it was concerned you were just about to. Apart from that one occasion it has shown no sign of aggression whatsoever.'

She paused while the rest of us mulled over what she had said, then went on, 'I don't know what it is or what it's doing here and I can't say that I like it. But I don't think any of those things gives us the right to attack it.'

107

'So what do you suggest we do about it then?' said Tina.

'I agree with Loki. I think we should take a low-key approach to this.'

'Low Key!' There were groans and explanations all around the kitchen as the penny dropped.

'We should keep an eye on it, twenty-four hours a day, and apart from that, for the time being at least, we should do absolutely nothing.'

'The Cat,' said Farral, 'has neither social nor moral integrity.'

'What?' said Nessa.

'He is lazy and indolent. He knows nothing of the value of industry or husbandry. He has no manners. He has no discernible moral code.'

Nessa's hackles rose and she stood up.

They were in the foothills of a range of mountains. The peaks that stretched before them were the biggest either of them had ever seen. They were sheltered by a steeply rising slope at their backs and the rain had stopped, but they were both cold nonetheless. Since the day they had met the fox, they had not lit a fire.

Below them a shallow valley stretched down through scrub and marshland to walled pastures, brighter than the other shades of green on the hillsides, but fading now with the coming of night. Nessa stared down into it, but she was seeing little beyond her own anger.

'Sit down, Nessa,' said Farral. 'I'm not telling you what I believe. It's what we're taught in my village by our parents and elders.'

'And what makes you think I might want to hear it?'

Farral thought about that for a moment or two. He was comfortable with Nessa now; they had been travelling together for more than a week. If he still had difficulty in finding words it was no longer apparent to her.

'I'm not sure if that's why I'm saying it,' he said. 'It might be one of the reasons. So that you know what you're up against. What we're both up against. But there's another reason as well.'

'Go on.'

'It's not easy to explain. For as long as I can remember I've helped out in my father's shop. Cats have always come in for haircuts and Dogs to get shaved. I never saw my father show disrespect to anyone. I know for a fact that he liked most of his customers, whoever they were. It was the same for me. Meeting you – and other Cats, too – is what started me thinking that the things I'd been told might not be true.'

He paused to lift a dead branch for Yorick, who dived in underneath it and gobbled up a family of woodlice, then went on. 'Sometimes it isn't really possible to know what you believe. No matter what you tell yourself. Some of those things get rooted so deeply in our minds that we find they're still there whether we want them or not. That's why the troubles keep flaring up again, isn't it? Because no matter how well we get on with our neighbours for most of the time, those poisonous roots are still alive deep down in our hearts. And when there's trouble, they grow and thrive.'

'All the more reason not to repeat them, I would have thought,' said Nessa. 'Why give them a chance to spread?'

'That's right, I suppose,' said Farral. 'Except that saying them to you is different. I thought it would be, and it is. It exposes them to another kind of light. I hear them as you hear them. Exposing them to you somehow takes away any last power they hold over me.'

Nessa shook her head. 'Sounds wishy-washy to me.'

'Try it then,' said Farral. 'Look at me and tell me what you've been taught about Dogs.'

'All right, then. Dogs are cowardly, both physically and morally.' Immediately Nessa could see what Farral had been driving at. Neither of those things was true of him. 'They are filthy beasts who foul everything they touch.'

She couldn't even smell him any more, now that she was with him most of the time. He might not seek out water as often as she did, but he washed from time to time. Filthy he was not.

'They hunt in packs because they are afraid to hunt alone. Their crawling hounds do all the dirty work for them. That's true, isn't it?'

'It is and it isn't,' said Farral. 'The fact is that most Dogs don't hunt at all. We're farmers or traders or craftsmen—'

Their attention was diverted by the sound of a band of grunts, squabbling amongst themselves as they settled down for the night. The birds had told Nessa and Farral that there were no villages for miles in either direction. It meant that there was little likelihood of encountering trouble, but it also gave both of them an increased sense of their isolation. The proximity of grunts, who tended to steer clear of any kind of settlement, was confirmation of their total dislocation from their own people.

For a moment or two they listened to the grunts, and then to the silence which fell as they sorted out their differences. Before it became too uncomfortable, Farral said, 'Anyway, what's wrong with hunting in a pack?' He glanced down into the darkness that had swallowed up the valley. 'I mean, as long as you're not the ones being hunted.'

'It's against God's law, that's what,' said Nessa.

'It's against *your* god's law, you mean,' said Farral.

'There is only one true God,' said Nessa fiercely.

Farral looked her straight in the eye. 'Do you really believe that?' he said.

It was a question that Nessa had never before been asked. Not even by herself.

2009

Saturday ~~Monday~~: February 23

Klaus is back, and it's just as well, because I need him these days. My biro ran out yesterday and I dug out a couple of pencils, but there's no sharpener to be found and the way I write I get through lead like nothing on earth. So now Klaus is my sharpener. I have three pencils and when one gets blunt he sharpens it while I blunt another one.

Anyway, where was I? For the first couple of days the Yoke just blundered and fumbled its way around the computer. One minute it would be studying the screensavers and the next it would be trying to find a way out of the third draft of Bernard's thesis on 'Spontaneous Genetic Mutation in Stressed Gerbil Populations'. But towards the end of the second day it discovered how to get the computer into DOS mode, and seemed to be in its element, spending hour after hour after hour trawling through mile after mile after mile of DOS programme files, watching the scrolling text with one, unblinking eye.

'It must have a phenomenal intelligence if it's able to understand that already,' said Bernard. He was there in the lab complex most of the time, whether or not it was his turn to keep watch. 'We should start a log. It's important to keep a record of what it does.'

'Why?' I asked.

'Well, for the sake of a case study, if nothing else.'

'Are you going to write an article for the New Scientist?'

'Ah, the New Scientist,' said Bernard nostalgically. 'One of life's lost pleasures.' I had forgotten that it wasn't being published any more. One of the thousands of things that was lost to us when the oil crisis changed our lives for ever. 'I might post it on the net, I suppose,' he went on. 'No one would believe me, though.'

'No one ever did,' I said. He had been soundly trounced by the scientific community for the first article he wrote about the missing link gene that he had discovered. They had rubbished him and his work. The only person who had taken a real interest was Maggie. She had begun a correspondence with him that had ultimately led to him joining her in Fourth World, and pursuing the experiments that had produced the talking animals.

Bernard sobbed dramatically into his sleeve. 'The tragedy! The misunderstood genius!' He went into the computer room and rummaged around in the book-case. The Yoke watched him while he rooted out an old reporter's notebook and tore out the first few pages, which were covered in his indecipherable scrawl.

'This'll do.' He returned to where I was sitting on a stool beside the door. He borrowed my biro, crossed out 'Retrovirus Culture' and wrote 'Yoke Log' on the front cover.

The eye disappeared.

Since Bernard's shock treatment we had gradually regained our confidence in moving around the computer room. Maggie's theory was proved right: as long as we respected the Yoke's personal space, it appeared to have no malicious intentions. In fact, as a Thing, a Blob, an Alien, a Visitor from Outer Space (any or all of the above), the Yoke was turning out to be a big disappointment. I had thought about life forms from other planets as much as anyone, maybe more, because of the ongoing speculations in Fourth World about the origins of the missing link gene. According to Bernard's extensive researches, it originated in the forerunners of modern man and was so unlike any genetic material that predated it that Bernard surmised it must have been introduced from somewhere else. His determination to find out how, or by whom, had led us on the crazy journey to Tibet to find the yeti. The trip had brought us no closer to answering that first, basic question, but it had led to conjecturing and, in my case, all kinds of imaginings. Some of the aliens I conjured up in my mind were nice, gentle, Spielbergian eggheads. Some of them were considerably less benign and gave me horrible body-snatcher dreams. But in all my wildest alien fantasies I never came up with a scenario like this one, in which an outlandish creature with spectacular abilities and intelligence arrives in our midst and shows absolutely no interest in us whatsoever.

'The concept of family is completely unknown to the Cat,' said Farral. 'Each year's young, born within a month of each other, are immediately orphaned. They are taken from their natural mother and passed from one nursing female to another. Cats have no parents, no brothers or sisters, no sons or daughters. They don't even have those words in their vocabulary. Instead they have uncles and aunts, he-cousins and she-cousins, nephews and nieces. Because of this they are cold and aloof, incapable of forming attachments, and dangerously individualistic and self-centred. They do not have the ability to love.'

Nessa borrowed the knife from Farral and cut the hare's liver into four small pieces.

'Dogs,' she said, handing round the pieces, 'are neurotically dependent upon each other. This is due to their upbringing, which takes place in the unnatural social grouping which they call the family. Instead of being introduced into the community when they are born, and therefore becoming everyone's niece or nephew, they are bound into a possessive relationship with their mother, her mate, and their other offspring. This small and stifling social unit fosters corrosive attachments and antipathies which inevitably spill over into relationships with others, both inside and outside their communities. Dogs set great store by what they call "love", but this is, in reality, nothing more than a distorted need to replicate their unwholesome childhood environment.'

The sting was going out of their exchanges of cultural wisdom. They had both noticed something very significant about the words they used. Nessa was coming to the conclusion that Farral was right. Bringing the intolerance into the open was exposing it for what it was.

'Do you know something?' she said. 'I haven't a clue what half those words mean. I just soaked them up without ever thinking about them. Lapped them up like milk.'

'Oh, milk,' said Bonnie.

'Oh, milk,' echoed Nessa and Farral together.

'You know how to milk a cow,' said Nessa. 'You couldn't steal some, I suppose?'

'I could, I suppose,' said Farral. 'If the cow would stand for me, which is unlikely. And if I had a bucket, which I haven't. And if there was a cow within ten miles, which there isn't.' He took the knife from her and deftly cut the hare into quarters. 'At least you're hunting again,' he said.

'Yes,' said Nessa. 'I'm beginning to feel like a Cat again.'

'I know what you mean.' For a while they had been so exhausted and disorientated by their long flight that their only ambition had been survival. Now that the urgency was behind them they were beginning to regain their strength and, with it, their spirits.

'I wish there was another word,' said Farral. 'A word that isn't Dog or Cat, but that we could use for both of us.'

'Grunts,' said Bonnie.

'We're not grunts!' said Nessa. 'Grunts are animals!'

'Watch your tongue, you little squirt,' said Farral to Bonnie.

Nessa experienced the old, familiar unease which surfaced every time she thought about grunts. She wasn't afraid of them as some of her cousins were. These days, walking through the foothills, she and Farral got regular sight of them, sometimes in fairly large bands. They were bolder here than in the more populated areas and often allowed Nessa and Farral to get quite close before they slipped away and found cover.

Nessa knew that they were gentle, timid creatures. Only under the direst provocation would they resort to aggression, and even then, like most forest animals, they would retreat rather than fight if they were given the option.

So it wasn't fear of them that gave Nessa such strong feelings of anxiety. It was something else. Something much more complex and sinister.

Farral was watching her, aware of her discomfort. 'Are you all right?'

'Yes.'

'Sure?'

'Yes.'

'There isn't, you know.'

'There isn't what?'

'There isn't any such thing as a talking grunt.'

Nessa nodded. 'I know.'

But Yorick, who had been dozing in the tree above their heads, chose that moment to make a contribution. 'I wouldn't be so sure if I were you,' he said.

2009

Sunday ~~Tuesday~~: February 24

This is what I wrote on the first page of the Yoke Log.

> 10 a.m. This morning it is still going through DOS programme files. When it first discovered them it went through them very slowly, line by line. Now it is scrolling through them much more quickly; almost page by page.
>
> 12.30 p.m. It found the Internet icon and hit the connect button but it couldn't get through.

That's because the server and the whole telephone network is completely useless these days. Maggie says we should be grateful that it's still working at all, the way things are in the country, but that doesn't help when you're tearing your hair out trying to get through. Then when you do finally get a connection, almost every link you make means you have to wade through floods of propaganda from the government and various anti-government factions. By the time you find what you are looking for the connection usually collapses before you can download anything. So I don't suppose the Yoke will find it much use.

> 3.10 p.m. It went back to the DOS files, finished going through them (I think) and went to sleep. That's what it looks like, anyway. All its arms

disappeared and it got shorter and wider and just sort of closed itself down, except for three eyes on three sides of it, which are just staring into different corners of the room.

4 p.m. It's still asleep. End of my watch. Tina is taking over.

Meanwhile, the everyday work carries on up on the surface of Fourth World, as if nothing else was happening. We got the broad beans planted and finished manuring the potato field ready for the spring sowing. Bernard got up a hedging party to do some trimming and gap-closing. But our minds were all fixed on what's happening down below. It isn't exactly enthralling watching the Yoke, but it's better than wondering what it's doing. Everyone's afraid of missing something momentous.

We have a kind of guard system. Two people watch the Yoke and one other, usually one of the birds or animals, stands up at the trapdoor, ready to run for help if there are any unpleasant developments. So far there haven't been any.

part
five

The birds brought disturbing news. Word of the murders and subsequent reprisals was spreading rapidly. Wherever it reached, it left its hearers nervous and brooding, anticipating the worst; preparing to strike pre-emptively if necessary. In some areas all male Dogs of a suitable age were required to enlist in their reactivated armies, and these began to drill, on horseback and on foot, as publicly as possible. There were rumours of at least two more grunt-kills. Large numbers of Cats were already abandoning their villages and setting up guerrilla camps in the relative safety of the woodlands. Several peaceful parties of Dogs, caught out after nightfall, had been attacked and robbed. Local Cats claimed that these were the acts of individual criminals and not acts of war, but talk like that made little impression in an atmosphere that was already brittle with tension. Initially, few casualties arose out of small-scale encounters, but it seemed it would only be a matter of time before the situation escalated. Already the trade paths were no longer considered safe, and communications between neighbouring areas were breaking down.

In all the reports that reached Nessa and Farral there were only two pieces of good news. The first was that the area in which they now found themselves appeared to be of no strategic value to either side. If things continued to escalate it might become a fall-back position for Cat guerrillas. It had been, apparently, in earlier conflicts. For the time being, though, it was as safe a place to be as any.

The other piece of news was entirely unexpected. Dogs had always employed horses, both gifted and mute, for farm work, transport and travel. When war broke out, horses of all kinds were commandeered by the army. Dog soldiers on horseback were a lot faster and thus a greater threat to Cats than those on foot, at least on open ground. For this reason Nessa, like most of her kindred, had an innate hatred of horses. But when she heard what the birds had to say that day, she was tempted to revise her opinions.

A group of four young starlings brought the story to Yorick. They were so excited that they could barely keep their balance on the branch where they alighted, and they were so eager to report the news that they all chattered away at the same time, which made it impossible to understand what any of them were saying. It was some time before they calmed down enough to get the story straight.

A Dog hunting party had gone out after grunts in the forest. The hounds had picked up a likely trail and followed it deep into the heart of the woodlands. Had they been successful, they would have paraded their trophies through the Cat village that they were intending to intimidate. Since they weren't, and since they were in poor spirits and fairly anxious about moving in the dark, they took a circuitous route, keeping to the farmland where they felt safer. It was here, on a path that ran between the trees and the pasture land, that they encountered a group of Cats. What they were doing there the birds weren't able to tell, but they must have been returning from the marketplace or on some other innocent business. They were not guerrillas; of that the birds were certain, because there were young ones among them. This, however, didn't deter the Dogs. Frustrated by their failure during the hunt, they decided upon a little intimidation of a different sort, and set the hounds on the party of Cats.

The gifted hounds stood off and barked. It was threatening behaviour, but it would have ended at that if some of the mute hounds had not misunderstood the intention of the pack. They closed in and began to menace the Cats more seriously, and two of them made an attack on a child.

The Cats, who were well-armed because of the prevailing tensions, defended themselves with clubs and pikes. The gifted hounds, seeing their mute kindred under attack, closed in and joined the fray. Within minutes, two of them were dead. The others, bringing the mute ones with them, backed off to a safe distance but continued to threaten the Cats. It was at this point that the Dogs, infuriated by the deaths of the gifted hounds, decided that the rout had gone far enough. But an astonishing thing happened. There were five gifted horses in the group, and when the Dogs urged them on into the fray, one of them said no.

The others, encouraged by the first, agreed. They announced, in no uncertain terms, that they wanted no part in that engagement or any like it. They turned round and walked away.

The mute horses, who were accustomed to taking the lead from their gifted companions, followed them. The Dogs were powerless to respond. No whip or spur had ever been used on a talking horse and never would be. Neither persuasion nor bribery, on this occasion, had the slightest effect. In a formation as tight and determined as any cavalry unit, the horses walked away from the war.

The Dogs, in utter disgust, dismounted and pulled off their saddles. They told the gifted horses that they were no longer welcome in their fields and barns and threatened them with all kinds of sanctions if they tried to return. The mute horses were frantic with distress as their friends turned towards the forest and disappeared among the trees, but the Dogs eventually calmed them and got back into the saddle. By then, though, the hounds had lost their nerve and rejoined the riders. The Cats, like the gifted horses, had vanished into the forest.

It wouldn't have been difficult to track them down, according to the birds. The desertion of the horses hadn't taken up much time and the Cats wouldn't have had much of a head start. But the hunters had lost heart. They turned back.

Nessa's initial delight at the news resulted from her relief that innocent members of her own nation had escaped terrible violence. But as time went on she came to realise that there was more to it than that. In terms of the conflict it was a tiny incident and would be of little or no significance in the overall scale of things. What raised her spirits was the realisation that somewhere out there in the evolving chaos there were others who shared their views.

Their views. Not just Farral's; hers as well. For the first time Nessa understood why it was that she was reluctant to return to her own kind. Farral was right; had been right all along. The causes of conflict did not lie in any fundamental incompatibility between the two races. Years of peaceful co-existence proved that, however different their cultures might be, Cat and Dog were capable of living and mingling in mutual trust and respect. The roots of the problem, as Farral believed, lay somewhere else, unseen and dangerous. He was right to try and dig them out. She resolved that she would go along with him, wherever it led them and for as long as it took.

2009

Monday ~~Wednesday~~: February 25

It was Maggie who had the idea of offering the Yoke a bite to eat. 'It has to get energy from somewhere,' she said.

Bernard was dubious. 'I'm not sure we want to feed it,' he said. 'After all, if it gets hungry enough it might let us have our computer back.'

'It might,' said Maggie. 'And it might come prowling round the kitchen in the middle of the night looking for the cornflakes.'

'In your dreams,' said Bernard. It was a long, long time since any of us had seen a cornflake.

'I could be wrong,' said Colin, 'but I can't see how anyone could be interested in cornflakes when they haven't got a mouth.'

'It might have a mouth,' said Maggie. 'It produces eyes whenever it wants them, doesn't it? Maybe it does the same with mouths?'

She was right, in a way, but she was wrong, too. As it turned out, the Yoke didn't operate like that at all.

Everybody wanted to be there to see what the Yoke's tastes were like, but Bernard wouldn't allow more than three of us in the bunker at any one time and we could all see his point. If the Yoke decided to get nasty it could probably wipe us all out in one fell swoop. So he went down to get Tina and Sandy from the lab, where they were on watch, and we had a mad kind of balloon debate where we all tried to make a case for being allowed in. It didn't work, though; it produced nothing more than arguments and sulks, so in the end we had to resort to more primitive means. We cut cards.

Maggie wasn't involved. She was practically barred from the lab complex on account of what everyone had come to refer to as her 'condition'. Bernard, predictably, pulled rank. Like it or not, he was going to be there. Danny was asleep. If anyone thought of waking him they weren't inclined to reduce their own chances by suggesting it. It meant that there were four of us competing for two places. Tina and I cut the high cards.

To soften the blow for the others, we devised a bet. Everyone chose a kind of food. Whoever guessed right about what the Yoke ate first would win the bet. The only problem was that we couldn't come up with anything to use as stakes. We don't have any use for money in Fourth World; there is nothing to spend it on. The little shop in the village only sells the most basic necessities: fish, cabbages, home-cured bacon, second-hand clothes. If there is any manufacturing still going on in Scotland, precious few goods make it as far as Bettyhill. Where food is concerned, the only thing that is in seriously short supply is eggs, and no one was about to deprive Maggie of her extra protein. We decided in the end to bet work. We all take it in turns to do the basic jobs in the house – cooking, washing up, cleaning the toilets and stuff. Whoever won the bet could off-load one job of their choice onto each of the others whenever they wanted to.

Enthusiasm doubled instantly. Bernard had gone below to keep watch again so Oggy went down to find out what his choice of food would be. The rest of us racked our brains and raced round the house and gardens, trying to come up with the best idea. When we gathered again a few minutes later we had a curious assortment of things on the kitchen table. There were two apples (one of which was quickly exchanged for a carrot), a bunch of wild flowers (a bit sorry-looking – not much around at this time of year), a pair of lobster claws, a small cheese, an AA battery and President Globalwarming.

'Was that Bernard's idea?' said Maggie.

'No,' said Oggy. 'The lobster claws are his.'

'Who put him there, then?' said Maggie.

No one owned up, but Loki was sitting under the table mumbling about 'motherwoes' and looking even more guilty than usual.

'I think she needs help,' said Maggie.

'Mayday,' said Loki.

'What's new?' said Colin.

'No, really,' said Maggie. 'I think she needs help feeding all those puppies. She's very young to have so many. Look how thin she's getting.

'Bingo,' said Loki.

We carried all the things down to the computer room. Since the animal members of the household weren't allowed to have a gamble, on the grounds that they didn't do any of the household jobs and therefore had no legitimate currency, Oggy elected to act as an independent observer on behalf of the players who couldn't see for themselves what happened down below. Oedipus was highly disapproving of the whole affair, accusing us of flippancy with regard to one of the most important discoveries ever made by rational beings. That gave us all pause for thought, which seemed to be all he wanted, because afterwards he consented to take the trapdoor-watch while the rest of us went down.

Thinking about it now, though, it does seem a bit mad. The thing is, it's amazing how fast you can get used to a situation, no matter how unbelievable it might first appear. The Yoke had only been among us for a few days, but in that time we had practically come to take it for granted. Maybe if it did more dramatic things we might be more respectful of its alien status. But when you've watched a thing do practically nothing for several hours every day, you just get used to it. Maybe it shouldn't be like that, but it is.

Anyway, we were hoping for a bit of excitement when we took the food and stuff down, and we did get to learn more about the Yoke. Oggy insisted that all the offerings be made together so the Yoke would have free choice. Needless to say, President Global-warming was no longer on the menu and the other six things fitted onto a coffee-table book of crop-circle photographs that was always lying around on the floor because it was too big to fit into the book-shelves. Bernard took it and crossed the room slowly with smooth, careful movements. Under the close observation of the Yoke he put the book down on the edge of the computer desk and returned to where the rest of us were watching, just inside the door.

Yet again the Yoke's reaction was disappointing. It closed its rearguard eye and returned its complete attention to its current preoccupation, which was a running through of the system's screensavers. It had got as far as the 3-D pipes and was watching the randomly produced shapes with intense concentration, as though they contained a coded formula for making gold. It looked as if it was going to sit there all day, but we stayed where we were and eventually our patience paid off. After the twentieth complex plumbing structure had finally self-destructed the Yoke returned to the screen menu and, quickly and purposefully, changed the start-up time from two to three minutes. Then, while it waited for the pipes to reappear, it began to explore the food.

It stretched out a feeler and grew some hairy little fingers, then followed them all with an eye on a long arm. It looked at and felt each thing at the same time; first the carrot, then the lobster claws, then the flowers. The cheese was the first thing to really take its interest. It felt underneath it, then rolled it over and examined every aspect of it with its eye. It even picked it up and seemed to show it to itself, like a bowler inspecting the new ball.

Our hopes rose. The pipes reappeared on the screen. The Yoke replaced the cheese precisely where it had been on the book and withdrew its arm and its interest.

We waited. It didn't watch the pipes for so long this time – maybe ten or twelve new designs and dissolutions – before it returned to the Active Desktop and reset the time-lapse to five minutes. While it waited for the pipes to reappear it took another look at the food. This time it focused on the battery and made a thorough examination of it, top and bottom. When it decided to eat it, it took us all completely by surprise.

'Eat' is another of those words that don't really quite fit where the Yoke is concerned. None of us could believe what we saw, but when we compared notes afterwards they all corresponded. The Yoke picked up the battery with four thin fingers and retracted the arm back into the formless bulk of its body. No mouth opened, there was no breach that any of us could see in the Yoke's surface, but the battery disappeared inside it.

I wish I'd had a video camera. What we'd just witnessed was impossible. If we had a film of it we could slow down the frames and get a better idea of how the battery went in. But we have no camera of any kind in Fourth World. It's one of those things like TV and telephone which Bernard and Maggie consider unnecessary.

'Colin wins, then,' said Tina, when we all got our breath back. But even as she said it, the battery returned. It came flying out of the nearest side of the Yoke, rolled across the floor and came to rest against Oggy's front paw. How it had come out, none of us had been able to see. One minute it was inside the Yoke and the next it was in the air.

'Maybe Colin doesn't win,' said Tina.

'It doesn't have skin,' said Bernard.

'It's looking at the cheese again,' said Oggy.

It was, and it went on to 'swallow' it in the same way it had 'swallowed' the battery. But the cheese took considerably less time to be rejected. It had barely disappeared inside the Yoke's body when it came hurtling back out again, hitting Bernard on the knee like a well-aimed cricket ball. He yelped and hopped around, causing the Yoke to open three large eyes – the closest it had yet come to an expression of alarm.

Bernard restrained himself. 'I swear it's got it in for me,' he said.

'What's going on?' called Oedipus anxiously.

'It's OK,' I said. 'The Yoke doesn't like cheese, that's all.'

'Does it like lobster claws?'

'Not sure, yet. I doubt it, somehow.'

There was a pause, then Oedipus called down again, 'Can I have them then?'

Between midnight and dawn Farral slept and Nessa hunted. Both of them then slept until mid-morning, when Farral got up and went about some daytime business until Nessa woke in the mid-afternoon. The remaining hours, between then and midnight, were their shared time.

They were safe where they were and, since there seemed to be no point in going anywhere else for the moment at least, they found a sheltered spot and made a more long-term camp. There were huge, ancient tunnels which opened here and there across the mountainside, but their depths were so dark that not even Nessa could see what was in them and both of them were too afraid to make use of the shelter they offered. Instead they made their home in a crease where two wooded hillsides angled steeply down towards each other and met on level ground. A rapid stream ran down from the heights and had carved out a series of deep, clear pools. Beside the first of these, beneath a close family of ash trees, Farral built two circular walls, one inside the other, with stone collected from a nearby scree slope. He was an enthusiastic builder but not a skilled one; the walls were unsteady and full of gaps, but they did serve their purpose. Once he and Nessa were inside the inner circle no draughts reached them. Nessa gathered branches and made a roof of sorts. It didn't keep all the rain off them, and nothing could keep out the pervasive mist, but by the time they had finished it was undoubtedly the most sheltered spot in the forest.

Nessa hunted over a wide area of the mountainside. Pheasants were scarce, preferring the easier pickings of the lowlands. There were plenty of crows, but Cats considered them to be scavengers, like rats, and would not eat them. Out of respect for Yorick's sensibilities small birds were also off limits, and the local hares and rabbits were unusually clever. Sometimes Nessa returned to camp empty-handed and bad-tempered, but they got by. There were always woodpigeons, fat and slow, and from time to time she would come across a few goats and track one of them down to its end.

They didn't light a fire, though. It wasn't because of the bad memories of the last one or the danger of being located. There were enough gifted birds in the area to make a fairly reliable look-out cordon for miles in each direction. They didn't light a fire because it was simply too wet. It rained more often than not; sometimes soft, windblown rain from the sea, sometimes a worse kind, which ambushed them from the west and seemed to fall in lumps from jet-black clouds. Even when it wasn't raining, they existed in an almost perpetual mist which lay over them like a dome, night and day. Everything was always wet.

Nessa was growing worried about Farral. He wasn't exactly ill, but he wasn't well, either. He was gaunt; every bone in his body shoved tight against his skin as though it were trying to break through. His eyes were hollow and there were constant dark pits beneath them. He got out of breath too quickly.

He never mentioned any of these things, but carried on in his usual, practical way. Any lack of physical energy was compensated for by sheer strength of will. He was clearly determined to say nothing about his health, but Nessa, now she thought about it, began to wonder how long he could keep on going like that. She realised as well that she knew why he was doing so poorly. Life in the forest suited Nessa fine, but not Farral. His biggest problem was the diet. His digestive system couldn't handle the raw meat. He was doing his best, chewing long and hard, eating as much of Nessa's kill as he could, but it was never much. Nowhere near enough to provide for his growing body and the amount of use he was making of it.

'It's worse for you,' he said one evening as they huddled against the inner wall of the shelter. 'Cats hate rain.'

'True enough,' said Nessa. 'On the other hand we're much hardier. You spend your lives in stuffy dens all crowded together, so you're not used to being out in the open air.'

She hoped that he might talk about the way he was feeling, but he just shrugged. These observations about each other's cultures and habits were commonplace now. Few things that either of them said had any effect on the other. They had been through practically everything already; all the slanderous folk-lore that each community had collected and hoarded. They had examined it meticulously, sorting out the occasional thread of truth that ran through the tangled mess of lies; applying new honesty to themselves and their habits as well as to each other. But they both knew, though neither of them said it, that they had taken that process as far as it would go. There was only one area of their separate experience that remained to be discussed. And it was the one area that neither of them, for reasons that were not entirely clear, was willing to enter.

Tuesday ~~Thursday~~: February 26

'It doesn't have skin,' said Bernard again as he laid the table for dinner. 'How could a living organism not have skin? What holds it together?'

Tina and I had stayed down in the lab to write up the food experiment and do our stint of Yoke-watching. It was still, three hours later, footering about with the screensavers. The only interesting thing it had done was to move the other bits of food away and inspect the book they had been sitting on. It even opened the cover and turned over the first few pages, but its interest didn't last long. Sandy and Danny were down there now, doing their shift.

'I wonder if it has internal organs?' Bernard went on. 'I should have taken a swab from that battery to see if it had any traces of digestive enzymes.'

'I doubt it,' I said. 'That cheese didn't go through a digestive system anyway. It didn't have time.'

'Where is that battery?' asked Colin. It was his turn to cook, which meant we were having his speciality, vegetable crumble. He had just put the first dish of it down on the table.

Bernard took the battery out of his pocket and handed it over. Colin inspected it closely, then put it in his own pocket. 'So if it doesn't have organs, how does it function? It must have a brain.'

Everybody thought about that for a moment, then Bernard said, 'What if it doesn't? We're obviously dealing with something here that works according to a completely different set of physical laws.'

'What if it is a brain?' said Maggie.

Colin put the other crumble on the table. 'That's what I think,' he said.

For a moment the kitchen was filled with the sound of scraping chairs and stools as we all sat down to eat. Then Colin went on, 'What if all its cells are the same? I mean, we have specialised cells in our bodies doing specialised things. But what if it doesn't? What if it operates under an entirely different kind of system?'

I hid my irritation by helping myself to the crumble. Colin is the youngest human (or part-human) in Fourth World. He and Bernard are as close as Siamese twins, and Colin has been soaking up science since he was born. He's a bit of a precocious brat as a result and he makes no secret of the fact that he considers Tina and me to be Johnnies-come-lately and very much junior members of the family here. The fact that he's the best cook in the place doesn't stop him getting on my nerves at times.

But Maggie is like Bernard; she thinks he'll be the next Einstein. 'Go on,' she said to him. 'We're all ears.'

'We're not,' said Colin. 'But the Yoke might be. All its cells might be multi-functional. Capable of collecting and processing information but also capable of joining together to make eyes and arms and legs.'

'Not ears, though,' I said. 'I don't think it can hear at all.'

'It doesn't make any sounds, either,' said Tina.

'That's true,' said Bernard. 'But I think Colin could be right all the same. It's a good hypothesis anyway.'

'But the cells still have to communicate with each other,' said Maggie. 'We don't know if it has internal organs but it certainly doesn't appear to have bones or muscles. It must have some kind of a nervous system, though.'

'Not necessarily,' said Colin. He was in the middle of piling crumble onto his plate but he dropped the spoon and jumped to his feet. 'I forgot to try something.'

He went off upstairs. The rest of us carried on eating in silence until he returned with the pocket torch that he kept beside his bed. He sat down again and opened it. There was a battery in it already and he took it out and replaced it with the one in his pocket; the one that had been through the Yoke. Then he closed the cover and turned on the torch.

Nothing happened.

'I knew it,' he said. 'That's what the Yoke eats. That's how its cells communicate. Electricity. That was a new battery but now it's empty.'

'Oh, yeah,' I said.

'It is! Look! The torch is dead!'

'Nice one,' I said. 'But it doesn't wash with me. Where's your proof that it was a new one?'

'It was! I tested it this morning!'

'No way in the world,' I said. 'We're on to you now. You're not going to win the bet as easily as that.'

Nessa was woken by a series of light taps on the back of her head. At first she thought it was a dream, and she tried to retrieve the comfort of sleep. It wasn't a dream. It came again. She reached up a hand and dislodged Yorick, who fluttered around in front of her face.

'Shhh, shhh,' he said.

Nessa sat up. Her arms and shoulders were stiff and sore from the labours of the last few afternoons. Farral had discovered a source of flat stones: a colossal hillside of them that tumbled from the overgrown mouth of one of the old tunnels. He was confident that if he chose carefully he could build a little house with a corbelled roof to keep the rain off them. The only problem was that the stone heap was a mile away.

Nessa wasn't at all sure that she wanted a house of any kind. She was only staying where she was because it seemed as good a place as any for the time being. She was waiting for something to happen, and whether that was an escalation of the war or an end to it she didn't know. It might even have been a decision on her own part that she was waiting for: to return home or to go somewhere else. Whatever she decided in the end, it wouldn't be to stay in these mountains.

But Farral wouldn't listen. Some instinct that she didn't understand was driving him. With her help or without it he was going to build that house.

It was brutal work. Cats were neither builders nor farmers. Few things in their lifestyle required hard physical labour.

It wasn't part of their ethic as it was for Dogs. But Nessa couldn't let Farral do it alone, given the state of his health. So every afternoon they fetched and carried, and Nessa did her share, adapting herself to Farral's slow but steady pace. It meant that she needed her sleep more than ever if she was to be alert enough to hunt at night. So her first reaction to being woken by Yorick was one of intense irritation.

'Come and see,' he was whispering urgently. 'Stay out of sight.'

Curiosity overcame Nessa's annoyance. Yorick flew on ahead of her and perched on the wall. His flight was still slightly erratic and he was taking care not to put too much stress on the wing, but there was no doubt that he was well on the way to a full recovery.

Keeping low, Nessa crept to the narrow gap in the inner wall. From there she could see Farral, crouching just inside the entrance to the outer circle, peering out at something she could not yet see. Bonnie was beside him, trembling from head to foot. Nessa slipped over to them so quietly that neither of them heard her. When she crouched between them they both jumped violently. Bonnie in particular seemed to be a nervous wreck, shaking like a cornered rabbit. It wasn't fear, however, that was giving her the jitters.

A band of about twenty adult grunts and a dozen or so youngsters were gathering beside the three pools, taking it in turns to drink. They were completely at ease and clearly had no idea that they were being watched.

Farral gestured to Bonnie, whose eagerness to chase the grunts was threatening to get the better of her. He pointed to the inner circle, from where the pup wouldn't be able to see and wouldn't be so sorely tempted. Bonnie resisted. Farral insisted. Still trembling, Bonnie slunk away and disappeared behind the wall.

Nessa turned back to watch the grunts. They had all finished drinking now but they were in no hurry to be on their way. Some of the youngsters started splashing in and out of the pools, playing in the water; sending fistfuls of it glittering into the grey air. They made that strange sound, so like laughter, and it brought on the old feeling of discomfort, so familiar to Nessa. She was repulsed and fascinated at the same time by their movements, their subtle animal communication, their nakedness. She had never before had the chance to observe them at such close quarters. Not alive, anyway.

The young ones' games became more energetic. They began to chase each other across the stream, jumping lightly from one side to the other. Before long the games spread to include the nearby trees. Some of the adults watched; others foraged, lifting stones and fallen branches to look for grubs and raking through the leaf-mould in search of fresh shoots. Nessa had given Farral lessons in patience and stillness. She was pleased to see that he had learned them well. He was practising the slow, regulated breathing that calmed the whole system. Nessa had taught him that nervous creatures – those who lived in fear of being hunted – could sense focused attention as clearly as if it were a beam of light. She had shown him how to watch obliquely from the corner of an eye or with masked attention. His eyes were narrowed now, as hers were. Their interest in the grunts was all but invisible.

But their bodies weren't. One of the young grunts, swinging between two bare rowan trees, spotted them. She stopped dead and others around her, noticing the sudden intensity of her interest, stopped as well, and stared.

Nessa thought they would all bolt but she was wrong. Instead they edged together, the adults gradually drifting in and gathering beneath the tree where the young cub still sat, still staring. They were, Nessa realised, as curious about her as she was about them. And they were coming nearer, inch by inch. She could see their eyes, so like the eyes of her aunts and uncles and cousins, and yet so different. Some indefinable quality was missing; not hidden but absent.

Led by two young adults, whose curiosity was getting the better of their timidity, the whole group was approaching. Nessa was gripped by anxiety. It took all her years of practice to keep her nervous limbs still and her breathing regular and shallow. It wasn't aggression that she feared; no grunt had ever been known to attack except under the direst provocation. If she stood up and yelled, or called for Bonnie, it would all be over. The grunts would be gone in a flash. What she feared was not conflict but knowledge. Some truth about the grunts had always been denied by her society and, she suspected, by Farral's as well.

The closest grunts, emboldened by Nessa and Farral's stillness, had come to within three paces of them. Their eyes flickered back and forth between the two faces, searching for signs of aggression. Their nostrils were in constant motion, testing the air.

'Come on,' said Farral softly. 'Come on.'

The sound of his voice made them hesitate.

'Come on,' he said again.

From the ranks jostling up behind, an elderly female stepped out, closely followed by a half-grown cub. They crossed the remaining space and squatted on their heels, right in front of Nessa and Farral. Farral extended a hand. The female observed it for a moment then bent to sniff at it. Behind her, the rest of the band were closing in, pushing and shoving for position. The female reached out and took Farral's hand in both of her own. She pulled gently at his fingers, turned his hand over, ran her strong, dirty nails along the lines of his palm. Encouraged, others joined in and Nessa suddenly found herself surrounded.

There were fingers on her face, in her hair, in her clothes, between her toes. A shudder of revulsion ran through her but there were other feelings, equally strong, which prevented her from reacting. The grunts' fingers were dirty; the nails were misshapen and cracked, but the touch they imparted was sensitive. There was no harm in it. More than that, it was communication; a recognition on the part of the grunts of the same thing that was struggling to come to light in her own mind. A small cub climbed into Farral's lap and, taking his face between her hands, turned it towards herself. She looked deeply into his eyes, then leaned forward and licked him on the nose.

He laughed. As one, the grunts leaped clear, surprised by the sudden explosion of sound. But they didn't go far. Their startled expressions made Nessa laugh as well, and a moment later the whole band joined in with their own whooping and chattering. For Nessa and Farral it was a moment of delightful revelation but for Bonnie it was just that bit too much. Her patience and self-restraint had been stretched too far. She hurtled out of the inner ring and into the middle of the grunt pack, barking and yelling at the top of her voice. The grunts scattered, some taking to the trees, others splashing across the stream and away. Within seconds they had all vanished into the mist and the forest was as silent and as still as if they had never been.

A thin drizzle was falling. Bonnie knew she had done wrong. She crept up and pushed herself between Farral's feet saying, 'Sorry. Sorry. Sorry.'

'Oh, Bonnie,' said Farral, but neither he nor Nessa could bring themselves to be angry with her. They were still amazed; still enchanted by what had happened. And the question that had been trying to form itself in Nessa's mind for as long as she could remember finally dropped out into the damp air.

'What are they, Farral?'

part
six

2009

Wednesday ~~Friday~~: February 27

This morning something happened that proved Colin was right yet again. I was on the early watch with Sandy – Maggie had dragged me out of bed at some unearthly hour – and to be honest I was finding it hard to stay awake. Watching someone use a computer, even when the someone is an Amazing Thing from Somewhere Else is a pretty monotonous business, especially when all it's doing is plodding through the C-drive files. Sandy went off to the kitchen to make a cup of coffee when suddenly something new happened. If I hadn't been bleary-eyed from watching yard after yard of Bernard and Maggie's research papers I might not have noticed. But I was sort of unfocused and that's why I noticed the movement on the floor, round about where the Yoke's feet might be, if it had feet. It was growing a feeler down there, the first one I'd seen emerging from anywhere below its middle.

I called Sandy, who came back from the kitchen and joined me. The new 'leg' sprouted a half-dozen delicate little toes, which began to explore the tangle of cables underneath the computer desk. They all ended at the four-socket block that was plugged into the wall. The computer was connected to the block, and so were the printer and the monitor and the desk-lamp. The Yoke made a careful investigation of all the leads, then three of its toes turned into hard little

147

wedges, like bulky screwdrivers, and levered out the lamp plug.

Throughout the time it took to do that the Yoke didn't stop what it was doing at the computer. It seems to be able to divide its attention when it wants to. It's the same when it opens an eye to watch us moving around the room – it doesn't close the one that's looking at the monitor. It must have (or be, if Colin's right) an amazingly complex brain. It didn't even stop going through the files when it turned its foot into a perfect replica of a plug and shoved it into the electrical socket.

I expected it to drop dead on the spot, or at least to light up and start crackling or something. It didn't. I thought I saw a momentary glow which reminded me of the moment the yeti first handed me the stone, but afterwards Sandy said she didn't notice anything like that so I suppose I may have imagined it. What we both definitely saw was that the Yoke expanded, quite rapidly, by a few inches all over, and became a slight shade paler. That was all. After about five minutes it removed its toes, carefully replaced the desk-lamp plug and continued trawling through the files as though nothing had happened.

'Looks like Colin did win the bet after all,' said Sandy. I had to concede, and now he's cock of the dung-heap again, going round with a smug expression as though he just made it onto the Nobel Prize shortlist.

I spaced off on my own for most of the afternoon. It was a beautiful spring day and I planted a load of garlic and weeded the onions, which are showing signs of starting to grow again. Darling and Hushy were full of the joys of spring, and I got my first chat with Roxy the fox since we had come back from Tibet. He's in great form, enjoying the wildlife despite the bad weather. But my mind was still in the bunker. What the Yoke had done that morning stayed with me the whole time, replaying itself in my mind. The Yoke's sudden growth wasn't like a balloon expanding, suggesting pressure within. Since it didn't have skin there was nothing to stretch or get filled up. Its growth was more like the way a dense cloud or a plume of smoke might expand, not displacing the air but mingling with it.

Those thoughts led on to a whole lot of others. It's very far from being clear yet, but I think I may be on the track of a theory of my own.

2009

Thursday ~~Saturday~~: February 28

I tried to test out my theory on Tina, but I didn't get far.

'You know the way it made itself bigger?' I said. 'When it plugged itself in that time?'

'It didn't really make itself bigger,' she said. 'Not that much bigger, anyway. It just kind of fluffed itself out a bit.'

We were making up a gruel mix for the pups: thin porridge with milk. I was pushing it through a sieve because the liquidiser had broken down. Bernard and Colin had both tried to fix it, but the motor was burned out. There would probably never be a liquidiser in Fourth World again.

'That's exactly what it did,' I said. 'Fluffed itself out. But how do you think it did that?'

'I haven't a notion,' said Tina. She remained deeply suspicious of the Yoke, convinced that, however smart it might be, it was up to no good. Of all of us in Fourth World she was the most reluctant to speculate. She also knew the least about scientific principles, which was one of the reasons I wanted to test my idea on her. She might scoff, but at least she wouldn't be able to shoot it down.

'Well,' I said. 'Do you think it could do the opposite? Kind of fluff itself down?'

'What are you on about?' she said.

Loki was watching us eagerly as we worked. She was drooling.

'It's not for you, Loki,' said Tina. 'Would you cop on to yourself?'

Loki turned round in a tight circle and resumed her muttering and slavering.

'She's just hungry,' I said. 'So would you be if you were feeding six puppies.'

'Well, I'm just about to,' said Tina. 'I'll let you know in a few minutes.'

'Anyway,' I said. 'The Yoke. It hasn't got a skin, right? As far as we can tell it hasn't got a fixed structure at all. It appears to be a loose collection of intelligent molecules that can take on any shape they want.'

'Do you think they can?'

'We know they can.'

'But any shape at all? Like a human being or a dog or something?'

'Well, maybe not that,' I said. 'That's kind of magic or science-fiction type stuff.'

'The whole thing is science-fiction type stuff, if you ask me,' said Tina. 'I haven't got a clue what's going on.'

I finished what I was doing and dropped the sieve in the sink. Tina sucked up some of the mixture in one of the pipettes we had borrowed from the lab. She squirted a few drops onto the back of her hand. 'Still a bit too hot.'

'Anyway,' I said, wishing she was a bit more interested in my theory, 'this is what I think. When it fluffed itself up that time it didn't really get bigger. It got less dense.'

'Less dense?'

'More space between its molecules. Kind of thinner, like smoke gets thinner, or a cloud.'

151

Tina began pouring the milky gruel back and forth between two pint glasses to cool it down. I never knew where she got her ideas from. I would never have thought of doing that. 'So?' she said.

'So what if it could become more dense as well?'

'More dense than you, you mean?'

There was no point. I gave up.

None of the things that Nessa had been told about grunts came close to answering her question. They were wild animals, she had been told; harmless but stupid. As long as they didn't encroach too far into Cat hunting grounds they didn't merit thinking about. A kind of tolerable vermin – no more, no less.

'They're so like us,' she said to Farral.

She would have liked more sleep, but the encounter with the grunts had excited her too much. They were on their way to fetch more stones for Farral's house.

'Like who?' he said. 'Like you or like me?'

Nessa wasn't ready for that question. It brought her back to the night when she had cut Farral's hair and realised that she could no longer see what distinguished him from a Cat.

There was more thinking to be done, and from Farral's silence as he walked along she ascertained that he was of the same opinion.

Their regular trips to collect stones had created a tidy little path across the forest floor. It worried Nessa. Dogs made paths; Cats didn't. It was a point of honour with them never to follow the same route twice through any part of the forest. Paths were avoided by game, and were too easy for an enemy to follow.

The lower slopes of the stone hill were overgrown with grass and nettles and brambles. They made their way up onto the higher slopes, where the slate broke through the thin soil and could be easily escavated. Nessa sat on the ground and waited, as she always did, for Farral to pick the stones that suited his building plans. They had to be flat on both sides and as close to square or oblong as possible. He had to prise them out of the soil and smaller rubble, and for every good one he found he usually had to drag out six or seven unsuitable ones. Yorick darted about as Farral worked, picking up worms and insects as they became exposed. In contrast to Farral, he was clearly profiting immensely from the lifestyle and was bursting with health and vigour.

While she watched them, Nessa mulled over the new questions. All her life she had been educated in the huge and fundamental differences that were said to exist between Cats and Dogs. She had accepted it all without thinking until she and Farral had begun to analyse the things they had been taught. Looking at him now, as he laboured to free a huge slab of blue rock from the subsoil, she could see that there were differences – differences in custom and philosophy; even in the method of their thoughts. But compared to the similarities, the differences were almost insignificant. When all the surface trappings were stripped away, Cat and Dog were the same.

And if a few more trappings were to be stripped away, another truth which lay even further beneath was there to be revealed. If Cat and Dog were somehow interconnected, then so, without a doubt, were grunts.

2009

Friday ~~Sunday~~: March 1

The Yoke did another amazing thing today. It has discovered the CD-ROM drive and has started going through the big stack of CDs that Bernard and Maggie have built up over the years. New CDs are as rare as hen's teeth now, but in the past they used to get heaps of stuff by mail order from one or two specialised scientific suppliers. Most of them they bought, and they relate to their own fields of expertise: genetic engineering and microbiology and such-like, but there is another rake of stuff which various companies sent out to them on spec but which they never wanted and never used. It was one of those CDs on the 'slush pile' that caught the Yoke's interest today. It's a collection of illustrated articles about radio signals, from basic walkie-talkie stuff to the most advanced radio-telescope technology. I can hardly understand the first word of it, but the Yoke went storming through all the different stages of radio development in less than half an hour.

After that it did the most amazing thing. It sent out dozens of arms at once and made this frenzied kind of search through all kinds of menus on the computer, then hit upon the A-drive. It tried to send some of the CD articles to it but the programme kept telling it there was nothing in the drive, so the Yoke hunted around and found a floppy disk, stuck it in and tried again. The file got copied. Then the Yoke took the floppy out and swallowed it.

The casing got ejected almost immediately, in several pieces. It clearly took the Yoke a bit longer to examine the actual floppy inside, because it was a couple of minutes before it followed, flying out like a miniature Frisbee and landing in the middle of the floor. But it had clearly come to understand it perfectly in that time, as it proceeded to demonstrate. It put out a new feeler and shoved it into the drive. The first couple of times it tried to copy the file again it failed, but the Yoke must have eventually succeeded in turning its hand into a perfect replica of the floppy, because the third time it tried the drive clicked and whirred and, as far as the computer was concerned anyway, the file was successfully copied. The Yoke downloaded a few more files, then withdrew the feeler. I have no idea how, but I'm certain that the Yoke now has that information stored inside itself.

We're doling out the gruel mix three times a day. It's a messy business but the pups are already getting enthusiastic about the extra grub. Loki still thinks it would be more efficient to give her the gruel and let her pass it on to the pups that way, but Maggie says it's better to give it to them. Loki's already getting four times her usual ration and she's still getting thinner and thinner. And when the pups are fed with the gruel she does at least get a break from them.

Electra's nose has been put out of joint, though. She alternates between being profoundly jealous; accusing everyone of giving preferential treatment to the dogs, and making sure that we all understand how superior she is because her kittens don't need supplementary feeding. The fact that she only has four kittens doesn't cut any ice with her, and Oedipus was caught red-pawed stealing some cheese in a brotherly effort to placate her. For the first time I understand why they call female cats 'queens'.

Nessa and Farral made several trips to the stone heap, then went on a less strenuous walk to do some foraging. Yorick was taking longer and longer flights now; strengthening the damaged wing and checking out the surroundings. He had come across a patch of little meadows and hazel scrub a mile or two across the mountainside and that afternoon he showed Nessa and Farral how to get there.

There were few hazelnuts; most of them had already been gathered by the local rodents. Gifted squirrels harassed Nessa and Farral as they hunted for the few nuts that remained, telling them in no uncertain terms that they weren't welcome in that neck of the woods. In any case, the nuts they found were mostly shell and very little kernel, so it was hardly worth going to the trouble of biting them open. There were wild garlic tubers among the hazel roots. Nessa and Farral filled their pockets with them and then, to the delight of the rodent residents, moved out of the scrub and into the open meadows to browse on the sour wild sorrel that grew among the grasses. They stayed there for a while in an unexpected spell of weak sunshine, while Bonnie teased the squirrels and Yorick caught up on the latest gossip in the trees. On the way back they all made a detour to the stone hill for one more load. By the time they got home it was nearly dark.

Farral sharpened the knife and set to work on the young goat that Nessa had killed the previous night. He cut thin strips of meat for each of them, gave Bonnie the bones and Yorick a piece of white fat from around the kidneys.

For a while they chewed in silence, but as Nessa's physical hunger began to be satisfied she became aware of a hunger of another kind.

'You said something once, Yorick, about the grunts.'

Yorick had finished his meal and was balancing on one foot, trying to wipe his beak clean with the other. 'Did I?'

'Something about talking grunts. You said we shouldn't be so sure that there was no such thing.'

'When did I say that?'

'Didn't you mean it?'

Yorick hopped down from the wall and perched on her knee. 'Just a rumour I heard,' he said.

'Where did you hear it?'

'I don't know. The forest is full of rumours. You wouldn't want to take any of them too seriously.'

'Why are you asking about it anyway?' said Farral.

Nessa told him about the insight she had reached earlier in the day; about Cats and Dogs and grunts being essentially the same species.

Farral shook his head, as she had expected he would. 'That's ridiculous. Grunts are animals. They're mute.'

'So are some of the hounds and the horses and the birds. But we still call them hounds and horses and birds.'

'That's different.'

'Why? Tell me why it's different?'

He couldn't.

'What do the rumours say?' Nessa asked Yorick.

'Just what I've told you. That there are talking grunts. Not Cats or Dogs.' Darkness had closed in and he was getting sleepy.

'Will you ask around? In the morning? See if anyone knows anything?'

'I will.' Yorick fluttered up into the highest branches of

the nearest tree. Nessa watched him as he plumped up his chest and settled himself in for the night. It seemed so simple, being a bird. She wondered how the grunts coped with the cold. No fur, no clothes, no sheepskins. They were a hardy breed.

'I can't get my head round that one at all,' Farral was saying.

'Why not?'

'Well, how could they possibly bear any relation to us? We're descended from . . .' He stopped, and Nessa didn't press him. She knew that he had been about to encroach upon the forbidden area that they had successfully avoided so far. But to her surprise he continued; determined, perhaps, to distinguish himself from the grunts.

'I am descended from Ogden.'

The name, which a Dog does not utter within the hearing of a Cat, fell into the darkness between them. Nessa made no reply. Instead she got up and walked downstream until she was well away from the camp.

She needed to wash. She needed to pray.

2009

Saturday ~~Monday~~: March 2

The Yoke is consuming information at an unbelievable rate. Bernard is down here in the bunker constantly, keeping the log up to date, writing down all the things the Yoke is looking up and trying to make a note of what it's copying onto its 'handmade' disk. Sometimes it moves so fast from one thing to another that it's almost impossible to keep track of it. If the computer wasn't limited in its speed I'd say there would be no way we could keep up. As it is, we miss the odd thing, but it's easy enough to see the Yoke's main areas of interest.

It went through several volumes of encyclopaedias today, still following up on the radio stuff to begin with, then going on to satellite transmission and imaging. It studied and copied satellite pictures of the earth but skipped over the moon and spent a long time looking through more detailed maps of the continents, all of which it copied. It had a brief look at the history of warfare but was only engaged by articles on ballistic missiles, the US Star Wars project and, again, the uses of satellite technology. To my disappointment it shows absolutely no interest whatsoever in art, religion, music, architecture or politics. If it has come from space to study the human race it is missing the point, as far as I am concerned. It seems to have no sensitivity whatsoever.

To tell the truth, I was beginning to get bored of it. That was why Danny and I put our heads together to devise a way of getting it interested in us. Since Bernard's attempt to talk to it we had all made similar efforts, a bit more cautiously. As far as we are able to tell it can't hear noises of any kind, unless they are loud enough to produce a significant vibration. Nothing that resembles an ear has ever appeared. But we know it can read and understand text. It has proved that by downloading enormous quantities of it. That's why we decided to write to it.

We had no way of knowing whether it could decipher handwriting but we agreed that the chances weren't high. Letters on a screen are one thing; scrawls on a piece of paper are another. There was an ancient laptop in Sandy's room that had been retired after contracting a nasty virus which had slowed down all its operations to a snail's pace. We knew that it still worked though. It is an open secret that Sandy has written several chapters of a morbid autobiography and a few dozen melancholy poems. She had a password on those files but the word processor worked without it and when we tested it we found that the battery still held charge.

We decided to keep it simple. One page. A few basic questions. Danny leaned over my shoulder and made suggestions as I typed.

WHO ARE YOU?
WHERE ARE YOU FROM?
WHAT DO YOU WANT?

It seemed enough to be going on with. If we got a response to those questions we could always ask it some more. We picked up the laptop and legged it down to the lab.

Bernard and Colin were on watch. The Yoke was still gathering information. It had found an atlas on CD and was studying and downloading maps.

'It knows it's in Scotland,' said Colin. 'We can't work out how.'

'If it came down from space it would be pretty obvious,' said Danny.

'It'd help if we knew how it turned up here,' said Bernard.

We still hadn't worked that out. The trapdoor and the garage had both been locked from the outside on the day it arrived. They were still locked when we came in and found it. Those are some of the facts that give strength to my theory, but I'm still mulling it over and I haven't tried to air it again since my attempt to get Tina interested.

'I suspect it has some way of locating itself,' said Bernard. 'Maybe based on magnetism or something.'

We showed him what we had done with the laptop. He was delighted with the idea. 'Why didn't I think of that?'

As he had done with the food experiment, he took the laptop and put it on the edge of the desk, the screen facing the Yoke. The familiar eye followed him, rested for an instant on the words, followed him back to his post at the door, then vanished.

We waited. And waited. No feeler appeared to check out the laptop. No eye inspected it. The Yoke just continued to pull up maps, enlarge sections of them, download and move on.

We were patient. It had been a long time, after all, before the Yoke had become interested in the food the other day. But when it finished with the CD it was working from and exchanged it for another one, we took that for a sign that it had not noticed the laptop and its messages.

Bernard crossed the room and, with great delicacy, pushed the laptop a few inches closer to the Yoke.

Again we waited. Again the Yoke made no response. It decided it wasn't interested in articles on the genetic modification of plant cells and changed the CD again. The next one, a collection of virology studies based on the Human Genome Project, interested it more. It resumed the process of trawling and copying.

Bernard tried again. He moved the laptop a fraction closer and altered the angle of the screen, just in case the Yoke hadn't been able to read it. He had barely taken his hand off it when the Yoke flung out a feeler, rested it briefly on the keyboard of the laptop, and blew it to bits.

Debris flew everywhere.

'Out, out!' Bernard shouted, herding us into the corridor. He pulled the door towards him and peered round the edge of it, watching. The Yoke just continued with its information-gathering as if nothing had happened.

But something had happened, and it radically changed our opinions. When the Yoke zapped Bernard that time we all accepted that it had acted in self-defence. This time it was different. The destruction of the laptop was a display, not only of hostility but of contempt for us and our concerns.

2009

Sunday ~~Tuesday~~: March 3

I went to sleep then, but it wasn't the end of what happened yesterday. We called a meeting straight away to tell everyone about the laptop and to try and work out what to do.

'We've humoured it for long enough,' said Bernard. 'If it has so little respect for us, why should we put up with it?'

'I'm inclined to agree,' said Maggie, 'but I think we have to tread very carefully.'

'We certainly do,' I said. The image of that laptop being obliterated kept replaying itself inside my head. The force of it was terrifying.

For once there was no one down in the lab watching the Yoke. It was now considered too dangerous.

'We're back to square one, then,' said Tina. 'How to get rid of it.'

'We're not quite back to square one,' said Maggie. 'At least we know a bit more about it. What it uses for energy, at least.'

'Are you thinking of cutting off the power?' said Colin.

We all knew that wouldn't be as easy as it might appear. The nerve centre of Fourth World's hydroelectric scheme is in the lab complex, beside the computer-room. Banks of powerful batteries are stacked up there around the walls, collecting power from the

165

turbines up on the hillside, some driven by water, some by wind.

'The house and the bunker are on separate circuits,' said Bernard. 'We could cut off the power down below and still have power up here.'

There was only one question remaining after that, but no one wanted to ask it. In the end, Bernard just answered it.

'I'll do it,' he said.

I suppose we should have realised that it wouldn't work, but at the time it seemed like a good idea. The plan was for Bernard to go in, turn off the switch and lock the door to the control room. He was so nervous about it that he spent an hour searching for the lab keys. They were in the drawer under the sink where they always were, but he looked at them three times without seeing them. When he eventually found them, he seemed hugely disappointed and stood in the middle of the kitchen for ages swinging the keys and saying things like, 'Well. There we are then. Right, so . . .'

We all gathered to see him off and the mood was sombre, as though none of us expected him to come back. He wouldn't allow anyone to go with him, even as far as the trap door.

'There's no sense in anyone else looking for trouble,' he said. 'If I'm not back in ten minutes, lock the garage door and stay in the house.'

A few of us were already beginning to have second thoughts about the idea.

'Maybe we should think again,' said Maggie.

'I'm sick of thinking,' said Bernard, and left.

He was back in five minutes, though it seemed like hours to us. His hands were shaking but he appeared to be unharmed.

'Dead loss,' he said. 'It's way too smart for us.'

Our last few tea bags were about two years old and had a dull, mouldy kind of taste, but they were still produced, ceremoniously, on occasions like this. Tina poured hot water onto one and handed Bernard the mug. He looked at the floating bag as if it were a dead slug.

'I turned on the torch first,' he said, then I threw the trip switch and the power closed down. Before I could even get to the door it had an eye in there on a big long creeper. I thought it was going to pulverise me but it just went straight to the switch and turned it back on again.' He sighed and poked at the tea bag with a fork. 'The mad thing is that even if I had got out and locked the door it would still have got in. If it can turn its nasty little paws into floppy disks and electric plugs it can certainly turn them into keys.'

We all digested that piece of logic. If it was true, and it probably was, it could explain how the Yoke got into the lab, and that didn't sit comfortably with my secret theory.

'So what next?' said Colin.

No one had an answer.

2009

Monday ~~Wednesday~~: March 4

We're back on watch again, but only during the daytime. The reason for this is that Bernard won't let anyone down into the bunker without him now, and even he needs to get a bit of sleep occasionally. He says we have to keep an eye on the kind of information the Yoke is gathering because it's the only way we can have a chance of finding out what it's doing here.

This morning when Bernard and Colin went down it wasn't at the computer. For a moment they thought it was gone, and Oggy came racing back to give us the glad tidings, but it turned out that it was in the lab poking around with the equipment there. It stayed there for about an hour, examining everything, then went back to the computer. They said it turned itself into a tube and moved like a leech, end over end. Very fast. They had to run to get out of its way.

When I took over from Colin it had managed to get hooked up to the Internet. It was working as fast as the connection would allow, downloading articles on virology. After a while the link broke down and it went to sleep while it waited for the line to clear again. When I left it was back on line, investigating global weather patterns: wind currents, cloud formations, that kind of thing.

It was pretty boring stuff to watch, but it didn't worry me. The virology stuff did.

We had a brainstorming session this evening to try and put together everything we knew about the Yoke. We gathered in the sitting room in front of the fire. The pups squirmed around on the hearth mat while Tina and I fed them.

'So, what do we know?' said Maggie. She was wearing a tight T-shirt and every now and then I could see the baby giving a good kick. 'From the beginning.'

'It appeared out of nowhere,' said Colin.

'With all the doors locked,' I said. Everyone glanced in the direction of the back of the house. We had locked the trapdoor, the garage door and the back door of the house. Loki's three brothers, the Dobermen, were standing guard in the kitchen but even so we were all edgy.

'It could have come from anywhere,' said Sandy.

'Why here, then?'

'Because we have electricity,' said Sandy.

'That could be it,' said Bernard.

The major cities still have erratic power supplies, but when the lines leading to rural areas get damaged no one ever repairs them. Bettyhill has no electricity. Only hospitals, military bases and government buildings have energy sources as reliable as ours.

'So it might have come because of that?'

I wasn't so sure. It didn't fit with my hunch, but I was still unwilling to voice it.

'Why?' Bernard went on. 'What does it want? Apart from the odd drink of juice, I mean.'

'And information,' said Danny.

'And information,' Bernard confirmed. 'Can we extrapolate anything from the kind of information it appears to want?'

We went through the log book. Radio transmission.

Satellite technology. Maps. Human genetics. Virology. Global weather systems.

'There's a lot of information there,' said Maggie, 'but I can't see any obvious pattern to it. Can anyone else?'

'It might want to send radio messages to its buddies in space,' said Tina. Despite having lived large parts of her life on the streets of Dublin, Tina had managed to see most of the science fiction films ever made. 'It might be like ET. It might want to phone home.'

Neither Sandy nor Colin had ever seen a film of any kind. Maggie and Bernard hadn't seen that one. Tina had to explain the plot, which took some time.

'It's a possibility,' said Bernard. 'In which case we might expect to see a spaceship landing in the hay meadow any day now . . .'

'The Yoke would have to find a decent radio transmitter first.'

'The maps,' said Danny. 'It would have found out where the radio telescopes were in the articles and then looked them up on the maps.'

'And the weather patterns and the satellite systems,' said Colin. 'That would all fit with trying to land a spaceship.'

'It's a possibility,' said Maggie, 'but if that's what it wants then why doesn't it just go off and do it? What's it waiting for?'

'Maybe it wants to study us,' said Tina. 'We're an alien life form, after all.'

'Speak for yourself,' said Colin.

'So what does it want?' said Danny. 'What's all this stuff about genetics and virology?'

Tina spoke for all of us. 'I don't know,' she said, 'but I don't like it.'

My ideas are getting madder and madder. Tina's idea about the radio transmitter has just added another bit to it. A sort of beginning bit. How the Yoke got here in the first place. It's nuts, but

part
seven

Nessa went into the forest that night as she did on every other, but any hunting she did was half-hearted. She was preoccupied with what had happened earlier in the evening and with how she should react to it. Despite all Farral's enthusiasm for breaking down barriers between them, it now appeared that he had created an obstacle to understanding.

Created it, or illuminated it? Perhaps it was her turn to take the lead for a while. But could she? Atticus was her foundation; not only the father of her people but the creator of the philosophy upon which her nation's identity rested. Without Atticus there were no Cats. Without God, was there any reason for existence?

Nessa found a nest of mice and spent much of the night lying in wait outside it. Her body was utterly still, but her mind sped backwards and forwards like a confused stoat, following the same dead-end tracks over and over again. She caught several mice; despatched them quickly; ate them all on the spot. She picked a pigeon out of a tree but missed a second one because her mind was not sufficiently composed and she lost footing on a wet branch. It wasn't until then that she faced up to the thing that was troubling her the most. The name of the false Dog god, Ogden, was known to all Cats but it was rarely spoken. She had never before heard it uttered by a Dog. There was only one time when either community spoke the names of their gods within hearing of the other.

That was during a declaration of war.

For the second day running Nessa was woken by Yorick's beak. This time she knew why, and crept straight to the entrance-way, where Farral was crouched again, watching.

The grunts had come back. They were taking the opportunity to drink at the stream but there was no doubt that it wasn't thirst that had drawn them there. They were wary, keeping an eye out for Bonnie, but they were also bolder in their intention than they had been the previous day. They had come to pay Farral and Nessa another visit.

Nessa was surprised by how pleased she was to see them. Now that the reasons for her anxiety about them had become clear to her, she found that she was as fascinated by them as they were by her. She stepped out of the stone circles and into an open space between the trees. The grunts retreated, but only for a moment. As soon as Nessa stopped and hunkered down again they turned back and, with unexpected confidence, surrounded her. Deft fingers touched her skin, lifted her hands and turned them over, picked at her clothes. One of the females searched her hair for lice. Another, a young male, took it upon himself to trim her fingernails with his teeth. A small cub found a fat chafer grub in the leaf-mould and popped it into her mouth.

Farral joined her, moving softly. The grunts stood their ground and some of them turned their attention to him. They were fascinated by the teeth he wore round his neck and by the tattoos, which several of them tried to lick away, as though they were dirt.

Nessa began to return some of the gestures, touching and stroking and grooming, but stopping short of licking their weather-toughened skin. One of the smallest cubs climbed into her lap and pulled one of her arms around itself. It was an action that was familiar to her; some of her little nephews and nieces had done the same thing. It had always made her feel protective and proud, and this time was no exception. To her own, as well as everyone else's amazement, she began to purr.

For a while longer the grunts stayed, sitting and standing around Nessa and Farral like long-lost friends. Then, by some common decision that Nessa did not understand, they began to drift away again. The cub in her lap was sleeping. It was not a cub. As Nessa looked down at its peaceful, trusting form, she knew that it was a child. Apart from its matted hair and weather-darkened skin, it was indistinguishable in every respect from one of her own clan. Even the soft exclamation it made as its mother lifted it up might have been made by one of her small nephews or nieces. Only when it turned to take a last look at her did the resemblance end. There was a vacancy in its eyes. It had intelligence, but not of the kind that she and Farral had, and Bonnie as well, and Yorick. There was no way, Nessa was quite certain, that a grunt could learn to talk.

2009

Thursday: March 5

But Yorick had other ideas. He had been up since daybreak, following the grapevine, collecting what information he could. 'Most of the birds have heard the rumour, but none of them has actually seen talking grunts. I did meet with a starling, though, who said her mother had seen them. They're all passing on the word anyway. Beak to beak.'

He had already explained to them how the network operated. Each gifted bird had a maximum range of a square mile or so, but the ranges overlapped and most birds met friends and informants at various times throughout the day. From bird to bird news spread fast, travelling anything up to fifty miles in a day.

'Where are they?' Nessa asked.

'Up north, she said they were. On the other side of the Foul Land. At the end of the earth.'

'Oh, well,' said Farral. 'It's definitely true, then, isn't it? I mean, anything and everything exists up there, doesn't it?'

His tone was heavily sarcastic, but Nessa could detect the anxiety lying beneath it. The Foul Land, or the Dreadlands, as some of her people called it, was the end of the earth as far as she was concerned.

The elders in her village told the story. When the old world ended and the new world began, a monstrous explosion took place which rocked the earth and started a fire that burned for twenty years. For a hundred miles in every direction people and animals sickened and died, and the ones that survived gave birth to monstrous offspring. Gigantic insects were spawned there, and all manner of terrible creatures. The people who lived south of the poisonous area mounted guards and slaughtered every living thing that emerged, whether it looked normal or not. A high wall was built across the land. No one went north of that wall. It was the end of the world.

'How could they know?' said Nessa. 'How could anyone see anything on the other side of the Foul Land when no one goes there?'

'Birds go there,' said Yorick. 'And animals, too, now. The wall is still there but there are no guards any more. No one goes to the worst areas, but there are other parts of it that are safe now, over to the east. They're just like anywhere else, except that no Cats or Dogs live there.'

'It's just a story, Nessa,' said Farral. 'There's no point in getting your hopes up about it. There's nothing beyond the Foul Land. Everybody knows that.'

Nessa spoke before she had even thought about what she was saying. 'Who is everybody, Farral? I used to know, but now I'm not so sure. Every Dog? Every Cat? You can't mean every gifted bird or animal, because they don't say that, according to Yorick. So are you saying we know best? Maybe we're wrong? Maybe it's just another of those stories we've been told?'

Farral, for a change, was on the defensive. 'What if it is? You're not suggesting we go traipsing into the Foul Land, are you?'

She wasn't. Nothing had been further from her mind when she began to speak. But her blood was boiling; not just because of the stance Farral was taking now. It was because of what he had said the night before. Because he had spoken the name of the Dog god in her presence. In the grip of that anger she found herself blundering into uncharted territory.

'Why not?' she said. 'If the birds and animals say it's safe, why shouldn't we believe them?'

'Well, even if we do believe them, so what? What's so important about this business of the talking grunts anyway?'

Nessa didn't answer. She looked around at the place that had become their home. Farral had been working on the house that morning while she slept. The walls he was building with the new stones were beautifully made, but they didn't yet reach much higher than her knees. It would take months to carry enough to finish the house. And assuming that they succeeded in doing that, then what? How long did he expect them to stay there? What was the point?

She walked away downstream to a place where she could wash and pray in peace. Alone, with her own quiet thoughts, she knew what she wanted to do. She wanted to go home, to live as she had always lived with her own clan, in peace. But there was no peace. Peace was gone. Until it returned she could not go home. She did not even know whether home existed any more.

When she returned to the camp, Farral and Bonnie were gone, on their first trip to the stone heap of the day. Nessa plucked and cleaned the pigeon while she waited for them to come back. Yorick sat on her shoulder.

'Do you believe it, Yorick?' she asked him. 'About the talking grunts?'

'A lot of the birds are certain they exist,' he said. 'There are a few dissenters as well, who say that they're just Cats with long hair or Dogs with no tattoos. But there are so many reports. They can't all be made up.'

Nessa finished what she was doing and lay down to catch up on some sleep. When she woke it was approaching dusk, and she was relieved that it was too late for her to go with Farral for stones. It meant that she didn't need to decide whether or not she would do it. Today or any other day.

Farral looked pale and exhausted. 'Sleep well?' he said, a little irritably.

That, she realised later, was the moment she decided. Or

perhaps it had happened earlier, while she slept. At any rate, she knew. 'I suppose the birds would help us find the way across the Foul Land,' she said to Yorick. 'Assuming you're coming along, that is.'

'Wait,' said Farral. 'Wait a minute. What's happening? We haven't talked about this.'

'There's nothing to talk about. I'm going to look for the grunts, that's all.'

'But you can't! This is a safe place. We're building a house. I mean, who knows what's happening' – he gestured wildly with his hand, taking in every direction there was – 'out there?'

Nessa knew how cold her eyes could appear when she turned a hard stare on someone. She didn't care. 'I didn't ask you to come with me. Build your little house if that's what makes you happy.' She could see how much her words hurt him and felt a twinge of regret.

'This is because of what I said yesterday, isn't it? About . . . about . . .' He couldn't bring himself to say the name again. 'I didn't mean to offend you, you must know that. I knew I shouldn't say it. That's why I did. It was like all the other Cat/Dog stuff. I wanted to know how it would sound.'

Nessa hesitated, struggling with a flurry of emotions. She wanted to be free of him and the sense of responsibility she was beginning to feel towards him. And yet she was drawn to him in a way that she had only ever experienced among her own kindred. As well as that, there was a part of her that wanted to keep working with him; not in building his foolish house, but in exposing the hidden hearts of their cultures; stripping them both down until all that remained was . . . Was what?

Talking grunts?

The thoughts disturbed her. She avoided them; picked up her sheepskin. 'You coming, Yorick?'

But Yorick never had to choose between his two friends.

'Wait, Nessa,' said Farral. 'If we're going to do this, let's do it right. Let's travel by day, so Yorick and his friends can keep watch.'

'You're coming with me?' she said.

'Don't you want me to?'

She was tempted to say no, but it would have been a lie.

2009

Friday: March 6

Their departure in the morning was delayed by the early arrival of the grunts, coming for yet another visit. Already Nessa was beginning to recognise individuals in the group: the mother of the small cub who had sat on her lap; the youngster who had given her the grub to eat; a mature male, more reticent than some of the others, who had a face that Nessa would have considered handsome had he been a Cat.

The visit was similar to the last one. Bonnie was reluctantly gaining control over her instincts and behaved with admirable restraint. There was a lot of touching and grooming; a gift, to Farral this time, of a bulb of wild garlic; then a gradual drifting away of the grunts to their forest life. Nessa was sorry to see them go.

But she was delighted, soon afterwards, to be on the move again. Cats prided themselves on their attachment to place; although they never claimed to own land, as Dogs did, they were fiercely possessive of their hunting ranges and the forests that contained them. Although Dog buildings were more permanent than the tree houses that Cats built, the populations of Dog settlements were far more fluid, with labourers coming and going according to the seasons and regular intermarriages between far-flung villages. Cats, on the other hand, though they would travel great distances in search of a suitable mate, always returned to their home places.

But now that the pressure of pursuit was no longer with her, Nessa found that she loved the adventure of travelling into the unknown. By midday they had passed beyond the outermost limits of her hunting grounds and were moving through new territory; forests choked with rhododendrons and littered with small, dark lakes. It was wild country, full of game; safer even than the sparser woodland they had left behind. Only one thing puzzled Nessa. She had assumed that the Foul Land lay to the north, but they had not taken a northward step all day. As far as she could determine, they had been heading due east.

'North leads straight into the sea,' Yorick told her. 'In any case we'll be heading east and north-east for a good few days if we want to stick to the safer parts of the Foul Land.'

Nessa left it to him and his network of informants. It was well accepted that no one knew their way about the world like the birds did.

That night, despite the proliferation of game in the area, Nessa didn't hunt. What remained of the kid was enough for the four of them, and Nessa was more than ready for sleep after the day's hike. There was, she and Farral decided, no need for a fixed plan. They were in no particular hurry. Nessa would hunt when they needed meat. They would move on as and when it suited them.

They slept in a rhododendron thicket so dense that it kept nearly all the rain off them. All four of them were tired enough to sleep as soon as they'd eaten. At least, Nessa thought as she drifted off to sleep, there would be no grunts arriving to wake her in the morning.

She was wrong. It was Bonnie who heard them and woke the others. For the fourth day running they were receiving a morning call.

'I don't believe it,' said Farral, as the familiar faces began to emerge from the surrounding undergrowth. 'It's the same band. They've followed us.'

2009

Thursday ~~Saturday~~: March 7

What a mess. What a mess. I haven't slept for two nights and I still can't sleep. I'm so scared. I'm down in the kitchen. We're all down here except for Maggie, who has conked out from exhaustion on the sitting-room sofa, and Bernard, who is out in the garage. Nobody's talking apart from Tina, who keeps telling the rest of us to go and get some sleep. There's nothing else to be said. We've said it all and it hasn't helped. There's nothing to be done, either, but we still can't sleep. We just keep waiting.

I suppose it started the last time I was writing in this book. I heard someone talking outside my door and I went out to see what was happening. It was Tina and Colin and they didn't look pleased to see me. It was quite obvious that they were conspiring together about something but they denied it; they wouldn't let me in on it. When they both went into Tina's room, I should have known something was up. I should have followed them, or told Maggie and Bernard, or at least kept an eye on them. But I didn't. I got into a huff and went to bed.

I don't know if the gunshot woke me or if I just built it into the story afterwards. What I remember for sure is every dog in the place, inside and outside, screaming and barking. Loki was at my door before I could cross the room to open it, shouting about

Armageddon and apocalypse. Bernard was already on the landing and the others emerged as we raced for the stairs. When we got to the kitchen Tina was coming in through the back door. She was as white as the wall and shaking like a leaf.

'Colin,' she said. 'Oggy. It's got them.'

Bernard ran out, yelling at the rest of us to stay where we were, but we all tore out after him anyway. The garage door was open but the trapdoor was closed. Bernard tried to open it but it was locked. I ran in for the keys but they weren't there. Tina said Colin had them. Maggie said she knew where there was a spare set, and went off to get them.

When I got back out, Bernard was shouting through the closed door and, to my relief, Colin was answering. He was frightened but OK. The Yoke had grabbed him and shut the two of them in but it hadn't hurt either of them. It had given him a tiny prick on his leg, he said. That was all. Like a needle. Didn't hurt at all.

At that moment it looked as if everything might turn out all right. But when Maggie came in with the spare key it wouldn't work. It wouldn't even go into the hole.

'It's the wrong flaming key!' said Bernard.

'It's not,' said Maggie. 'It's labelled – look.'

Bernard tried a couple of the other keys but none of them would go in. It wasn't until he shone a torch into the keyhole that he realised what had happened. 'It's blocked it,' he said. 'Colin?'

Colin's voice came back, thin and worried. 'Yes?'

'Is there something in the keyhole on your side?'

'No. But the Yoke stuck a feeler in it when it closed it up.'

Bernard swore under his breath and spoke quietly

so Colin couldn't hear him. 'It's fused it. Melted the whole flaming mechanism.'

'Dad?' said Colin.

'Yes?'

'Can you get us out?'

'Of course we can. What's the Yoke doing now?'

'I don't know,' said Colin.

'It's on the Internet,' said Oggy. 'Looking at stuff about dogs, of all things.'

'Dogs?' said Maggie.

Loki was standing beside me. She'd been practically glued to my left leg since I'd come out of my bedroom door.

'Jigsaw,' she said.

'Bit of a puzzle all right,' I said.

'What the hell do we do now?' said Bernard, under his breath.

'Jigsaw,' said Loki again.

I shushed her. I hadn't realised she was thinking ahead of us all.

'She's right,' said Sandy. 'Cut out the lock with a jigsaw!'

The tools were in the garage.

'The drill first,' said Sandy, who was Fourth World's master carpenter.

We dug it out and the jigsaw and the extension lead. The top of the trap door was disguised with a nailed-down trunk and old rags and stuff, to make it look like a messy part of the garage floor. While Sandy and I sorted out the right drill bit and fitted it, Bernard and Tina wrenched out the trunk and cleared the rags away from the area around the lock. When the drill was ready Bernard grabbed it, but his hands were so unsteady that he relinquished it to me without objection when I offered to take over. I positioned the drill and turned it on. It went through the wood in no time and I was just about to pull it back when a huge shock threw me backwards across the floor of the garage. The drill landed beside me, and although I was completely dazed I had enough of my wits about me to scramble up and get as far away from it as possible. There was no need, though. The shock had blown the trip switch. The garage light had gone out.

Bernard turned on the torch and found me with the beam.

'You all right?' said Maggie.

I still wasn't quite sure, but I nodded. She came over and gave me a hug; no mean feat with the bulge in the way.

Bernard was calling through the door. 'Colin?'

'It touched the end of the drill,' said Colin. 'There was a big flash. Are you OK?'

'Christie got a shock but he's all right. What's happening down there?'

'Nothing,' said Colin. 'It didn't even come out of the computer room. Just sent out a feeler. Don't try it again, Dad.'

I doubted whether there was any point. The drill bit was misshapen like a piece of plastic that had got too close to the fire. But Bernard wasn't going to be so easily deterred. He reached for the sledge-hammer that was leaning up against the wall.

'Stand clear, Colin,' he called. He hefted the sledgehammer but the Yoke was ahead of him. Through the hole that I had so considerately drilled for it came a thin feeler with a lens on the end. The instant it spotted Bernard it snaked out towards him with ferocious speed.

He dropped the sledgehammer and ran. He didn't

need me to tell him what it felt like to be zapped by the Yoke. The feeler receded but a short length of it remained, complete with its eye, on watch.

I don't remember ever feeling so helpless in my life.

part
eight

Whether Nessa and Farral liked it or not, the grunts were going with them. They didn't see them during the day and Nessa never came across them by night, but every morning they appeared with the sun.

For three days the little group and their unseen followers travelled due east. The weather got drier but it also got colder. On the third day they descended from the rhododendron-filled woods into an area more like their own home forests. The trees were taller and broader and there was a wide variety of roots and shoots to browse on as they walked.

But they were also moving closer to populated areas. Yorick was busy all day, securing the help of the local birds and gathering information from all quarters. War, they were told, had not yet broken out but appeared to be imminent. Dog armies were mustering and manoeuvring in provocative ways. Cat guerrillas were setting up camps in the forests and hills, moving by night, liaising with groups from other villages. The marketplaces were full of cold silence and mistrust. The trade paths were practically empty.

There was talk, as well, of unrest of a more heartening nature. A herd of mute horses in a field beside a Dog training camp was found missing one morning. The soldiers accused the local Cat community of concealing them somewhere and terrorised several villages in an attempt to find out where they were. When the horses were eventually tracked down, miles away from the camp, it took two dozen foot soldiers several hours to herd them out of the forest and into a nearby field. It wasn't until then that a number of the horses broke away from the rest and jumped out over the gate. Most of them made it back to the forest and freedom but one, a gifted horse, lost his footing as he landed and badly damaged a tendon. He was far too lame to evade the Dogs now, and when they caught him he made no attempt to conceal the truth. It was gifted horses, on their own initiative, who had freed their mute cousins in order to keep them out of the developing conflict.

Nessa and Farral were delighted by the story. It had been related to them by a magpie who had been curious to see the horse's fate and had followed it through to the end. The horse was returned to the Dog family on whose land he had been born and reared. Despite his disloyalty the family didn't reproach him but took him in, treated his injury and made him comfortable.

The magpie appeared to be moved by the events. She believed that the Dogs were badly unsettled by the increasingly widespread withdrawal of the horses' support, and not only for logistical reasons. The relationship between Dogs and horses was an old and important one and, as far as anyone knew, it had never been threatened before.

Nessa took an immediate liking to that bird and persuaded her to stay around and talk some more. Her name was Brockle and it seemed to Nessa that she was a lot more thoughtful and observant that any of the other birds they had yet encountered. She was not only a wonderful gatherer of information but a good analyst of it as well. She had little time for the species barriers that divided the gifted communities. Whereas most birds kept themselves to themselves, Brockle would, as she put it, talk to anyone who would listen and listen to anyone who would talk. There were plenty of creatures who didn't have the gift of language, she said. Those fortunate enough to have inherited it had a duty to make the most of it.

2009

Friday ~~Sunday~~: March 8

I flaked out, finally, at the kitchen table and when
Danny came in, smelling of the sea, he ordered me up
to bed. But I didn't sleep well. I dreamed that I was
sitting beside the trapdoor in the garage and talking
to Colin. He was giving me the recipe for vegetable
crumble and it was amazingly complicated – all kinds
of waffle about carrots in test tubes and incubation
periods and mad stuff like that. I was trying to write
it out as a mathematical formula when the trapdoor
suddenly blew off its hinges and the end of the
world came out of the bunker. I can't remember what
the end of the world looked like, but I was in a
lather of terror when I woke up.

Anyway, back to where I was. Later that first night,
Tina told us what had happened. She was in an
awful state – almost paralysed by shock and guilt
and fear. Every sentence was preceded and followed
by apologies and regrets, but no one blamed her. It
was too late and too serious for that.

It seems that I wasn't the only one to have had
something hidden under my mattress. Tina had
found the rifle tangled up in her bedclothes after
the gang of invaders made their hasty retreat from
Fourth World. She knew that Maggie disapproved of
guns but she wanted it; it made her feel powerful

and safe. She hid it and sometimes, late at night, she took it out and examined it. She figured out how it worked and discovered that it was loaded. That was why she had made the suggestion about shooting the Yoke. No one else knew that there was a gun in Fourth World.

That night, on the landing outside my door, she had let Colin in on the secret. They had agreed not to tell anyone because they were certain that Maggie wouldn't allow them to use the gun. So they hatched the plan to do it themselves, in the expectation that they would be heroes after the event.

They waited until Danny had gone out fishing and everyone else was asleep, then they crept downstairs. The only problem was that they couldn't get out without passing Oggy, who was in his usual position on guard inside the back door. He tried to put them off but they managed to talk him into standing guard at the trapdoor.

Tina burst into tears at the thought. Life has been hard on her. Until she met Danny and me her mistrust of the human race was absolute. Even though she looks upon the Fourth World people as the closest thing to a real family she ever had, she is still, in some ways, more engaged with the animals than she is with us. She is the one who looks after them all when they're born and teaches them to speak. She does a great job and she's adored by all her pupils, but Oggy is still her first and favourite friend. It was he who met her in the streets of Dublin all that time ago. It wasn't because of Danny and me that she made the dangerous journey to Fourth World, but because of Oggy. And now she has got him, as well as Colin, into terrible danger.

It had just seemed so straight forward, she told us. She hates physical violence – she's seen more of it than most of us – but at the same time she believed that the person who had the biggest gun was always the winner in the end. It wasn't just the movies that had convinced her of that. It was, in her opinion, the way the world worked, pure and simple. And this time, she was the one who had the gun.

She led the way down into the bunker. Oggy stayed at the top of the stairs. The Yoke was, as usual, in front of the computer. She couldn't remember what it was looking at – she wasn't interested. She just wanted to do what she had gone down there to do. They moved very slowly and furtively and the Yoke paid no attention to them. She didn't think it had noticed they were there. She stood in the corridor with her back to the wall, the way people do in films, and slipped the safety catch off the rifle. Then she turned into the doorway, took aim and fired.

The Yoke opened an eye and watched her as she shot at it, but it didn't make any attempt to stop her. When the bullet hit it, it went cloudy for a moment, the way it had done when it was feeding from the electricity supply. Apart from that it did nothing at all.

Tina said they should have got out there and then, but they were rooted to the spot, unable to believe that the rifle shot hadn't damaged the Yoke at all. She said she still thought it might suddenly collapse or disintegrate. It didn't. After a moment or two it shot her back. It expelled the bullet the way it had expelled the cheese and the battery and the floppy disk, except that this time it used a bit more force. It had a good aim as well. The bullet hit Tina on the forehead, just above the hairline. We could all feel the lump it had made. Maggie said she was lucky that the Yoke hadn't thrown it any harder.

In any event, it was hard enough to knock Tina backwards, out of the doorway. She was still trying to get
her bearings when it lashed out a feeler, like a rope,
she said, and grabbed Colin by the wrist. He yelled and
screamed. Oggy came flying down to the rescue but
Tina didn't even stop to think. She bolted for the stairs
and up into the garage. She was barely clear of the
trap door when it slammed behind her, brought down by
a force an awful lot stronger than gravity.

The rest we knew.

We've all done our best to try and console Tina but
it's no use. She doesn't want to hear anyone else
saying that they would have done exactly the same
thing in her position; or that it would be worse, not
better, if there were three of them stuck down
there instead of two. She feels entirely responsible
for what has happened and is tormented by the fact
that she isn't down there with the other two, sharing
their fate.

But at least their fate isn't treating them too badly,
so far at least. The Yoke hasn't paid them the
slightest bit of attention since it first took them prisoner and pricked Colin in the leg. Oggy says it's asleep
most of the time, or appears to be. Meanwhile he and
Colin have the run of the place. Colin has been
cooking up gourmet meals. Oggy says he has never
eaten so well.

But the Yoke did a really weird thing this morning,
which has everyone a bit freaked out. It still has
the feeler in the hole that the drill made, and at
some stage it started threading more of them, so
fine that we thought at first they were hairs, or
wires, through all the little gaps and cracks in the
trapdoor. Then it wove them all together into this

weird kind of wiry dome which completely covers the door. We don't know why, but Bernard thinks it's probably made a perfect seal, completely airtight. We can still hear Colin through it, but not so distinctly. Naturally, no one has volunteered to touch it. Bernard tried throwing a hammer at it but it just bounced off, as if it had hit a beach ball.

'Why?' is the awful question. There was another thing as well, a couple of hours later. Bernard and I were in the garage at the time and Oggy was keeping us posted.

'Colin's asleep,' he told us. 'And the Yoke is too, though it woke up for a moment or two a while ago.'

'What did it do?'

'Nothing, really. It just sneezed and went back to sleep.'

'Sneezed?' said Bernard.

'Sort of,' said Oggy. 'It didn't exactly say Aahchoo! but it snorted out a kind of spray; just a few droplets of something. Into the air.'

'Poor old Yoke,' said Bernard. 'Let's hope it's getting pneumonia.'

His tone was flippant but the look he gave me was full of concern. I got the hint. 'Don't worry, Oggy. I doubt if Yoke colds are catching.'

We carried on chatting for a while, then Bernard and I went into the house.

'What do you think it means?' I said. 'The sneeze?'

Bernard shrugged. 'I don't suppose it means anything.' But I know that he wasn't telling me the truth because he did what he always does when he has stuff he doesn't want to talk to us kids about. He went off to find Maggie.

That sneeze has some significance, I'm sure of it. I wish I knew what it was.

Yorick didn't hold with Brockle's theory about duty to language. In his opinion she talked far too much. But Nessa and Farral found her presence invaluable. She had raised four broods of chicks and a lot of her sons and daughters were still in regular contact with her. She had also, it seemed, done an unusual amount of wandering for a bird. She knew the surrounding area surprisingly well.

'North-east for a few more days,' she told them. 'You could go due north and get into the Foul Land a lot sooner, but it's safer to keep as far to the east of it as you can.'

'I thought it was safe now?' said Nessa.

'Not all parts of it. Not where the piece fell out of the sun. It's still deadly around there. You wouldn't see or feel or smell anything, but it would make you ill all the same. Not worth the risk, I'd say.'

'What's this about the piece of the sun?' said Farral.

'That's what happened,' said Brockle. 'When the old world ended the gods fought. Where their arrows hit the sun, pieces fell out of it, and one of them landed up there in the Foul Land and burned for a hundred years. I thought everyone knew that.'

'It wasn't a piece of the sun,' said Farral. 'It was a war machine. It made lights and fires in every village in the world, and it made weapons as well. Flaming arrows that could destroy a hundred villages at a time. When the old world ended there was no one to look after it any more, and it consumed itself and half the old world with it.'

Nessa had never heard that story before. She wondered how many other stories Farral had that were different from her own people's folklore.

'A war machine?' said Brockle, clearly fascinated. 'But why would a war machine put lights and fires into villages?'

Farral shrugged. In his community you didn't question the stories or the storytellers.

'In any event,' Brockle went on, 'north-east is the best way. It's going to be tricky enough, though, if you don't want to run into Cats or Dogs. Lots of villages on the way.'

Nessa was looking up at the sky. 'Is it possible?' she said. 'Could a piece really fall off the sun?'

'What's wrong with him?' Brockle asked Nessa. They had descended into a valley and crossed a rapid stream. Now they were climbing out again, up the steep side. Nessa stopped and looked back. Farral was sitting on a rock, his head in his hands. Bonnie was lying at his feet.

'He's just taking a rest,' said Nessa, knowing even as she said it that it was a long way short of the truth. Neither of them had mentioned it, but it was becoming increasingly clear that Farral wasn't up to the journey.

'He can't live like you,' said Brockle. 'Dogs can't live on raw meat. He needs bread.'

Nessa knew that the magpie was right. Cats ate bread rarely – on Atticus Day and other religious occasions. It was a special treat and the children always crowded round the communal fires where the flat, round bread was baked on huge griddles. The smell of it was as much a part of the feast as the taste. For Dogs, bread was a holy food as well, but with very different connotations. It was the foundation of their diet. Cats prayed as they hunted. Dogs prayed as they baked.

Although the bread each community baked looked quite similar, it was made in a very different way. Dog bread was forbidden to Cats and Cat bread to Dogs. To break that law was profane. In Nessa's village, a Cat who was profiting too well out of doing business with Dogs, or was in other ways seen to be growing too close to the other side was said to have 'eaten Dogs' bread'. It was just about the worst insult there was.

Nessa went back down the hill and sat beside Farral. 'Are you all right?'

'Fine,' he said, but she could see that he wasn't. The black-berries and damsons that had helped him along to begin with were all gone now. The few haws that still clung to the branches were good to pick on, but too many of them caused stomach cramps and laid you up for hours. If they could even cook their meat it would help him, but from what Brockle had told them they were already too close to habitation to risk lighting a fire. While Nessa was wondering what to do Farral stood up again and returned to the climb. He didn't stop until he reached the top but, walking behind him, Nessa could tell how heavy his legs felt to him and how much effort it was taking him to keep going. No matter which way she looked at it, she couldn't see him lasting much longer.

'You'll have to go back to your people,' she said, as they sat together in the damp darkness that evening. 'Even if it's only for a while.'

Farral had tried to deny that he was in trouble but, with the help of the birds, Nessa had made him face up to it.

'You'll have to use that idea about the hair. You could say you were taken prisoner. For a ransom, maybe.'

'You're a prince from the southern kingdoms,' said Brockle. 'The kidnappers sent your hair to your father, to prove that they had you.'

'That's a good one,' said Nessa.

'They didn't feed you,' said Yorick.

'I chewed through your ropes and you escaped,' said

Bonnie. 'You've been wandering in the forest for days, looking for help.'

'Weeks,' said Yorick.

'I pretended I was a mute hound,' said Bonnie, beginning to enjoy her role in the fantasy. 'I never said a word the whole time.'

'They'd be sure to swallow it,' said Nessa.

'No,' said Bonnie, bristling with excitement. 'I wasn't with you at all. I just followed you, keeping out of the way, determined to rescue you as soon as I saw my chance.'

'I need time to think,' said Farral.

Bonnie couldn't slow her imagination. 'All on my own. Fighting off grunts and mad foxes, staring into the darkness all night, trailing my friend and his kidnappers all day, using my amazing nose, never sleeping, never—'

Nessa put a firm but gentle hand around her jaws and held them shut.

Nessa had caught three pigeons and was on her way back to the camp with them when she heard the faint shuffle and scuttle of a mouse nest and stopped to try her luck. She caught two in a short time, killed them quickly and began to make tracks towards the camp again. The mice would please Farral. They would be good for him.

It was then that she caught herself. Farral was not a cousin; he was a Dog. She was, she realised, becoming far too close to him. She didn't know what had come over her. It was against her nature, against the whole bent of her culture to become sentimental about another. She was tying herself to Farral. It was dangerous.

She ate the mice herself, and decided to go on without Farral. She would help him find a village, then say goodbye.

He was awake when she got there, his face as pale as a long, narrow moon in the first thin light of dawn. As she came up to him he began to mutter strange words.

'Ogden protect me. Guide my steps. Keep my body from all harm. Fill my heart with your boundless love.'

Nessa stared at him, uncertain about whether he knew she was there. Bonnie stirred in her sleep and mumbled, *'Hear us.'*

'May your sun and your rain nurture our crops. May your bounty fill our barns and our silos.'

'Hear us.'

'From your own hand we receive this bread.'

'Hear us.'

He was more seriously ill than Nessa had thought. He was surely raving, in some kind of delirious state. All the same, her hackles were stiff and a quiet fury prickled in her blood.

'Go back when the sun comes up,' she said to him.

'I will,' he said.

'Yorick will spy out a village for you. You'll be safe there.'

'I will,' he repeated.

'Go back to sleep, now.'

No,' he said. 'There's something I have to tell you before I go.'

'Between the death of the old world and the birth of the new, the first Dog was born. He walked out of the ocean, and his feet upon the earth reawakened it. He is the father of us all. His name is Ogden.'

Nessa watched Farral as he spoke, torn between fascination and revulsion. The form of words was familiar to her but their use was repellent. It was as though they had been stolen and twisted into heresy.

Farral met her hard gaze with his own, level and mild, and continued. *'At his coming every hound, gifted or mute, worshipped at his feet, knowing their new master had come upon the earth.'*

A sound above their heads made them look up. The birds were waking and Yorick was warming up his throat with a few sweet notes. Brockle stretched her wings and scratched a flea-bite with her beak. Yorick shook himself all over, ruffed up his breast feathers and settled them again. 'Take a look around?'

The two birds took to the air and, in the silence that followed, Nessa realised that when Farral was gone she would be free to sleep up in the trees again. The thought made her aware of her exhaustion. It was a long time since she had last slept.

'Why are you coming out with all this?' said Nessa. 'I want to get some sleep.'

'There's no time left,' said Farrall. *'Ogden knew no fear. With his followers he covered the lands and made of the new world his kingdom—'*

'I don't like to listen to it,' Nessa interrupted. 'I don't like hearing it. I don't see the point.'

'Will you go on?' he asked.

She knew that she would. 'I suppose so. What else could I do?'

'I thought you might wait a while. If I had a few weeks in a village I could get my strength back. We could go on together.'

Nessa said nothing. In a few weeks it would be hard winter.

Farral knew what her silence meant. *'From our father's loins the Dog nation sprang. From his mouth came all our learning. From his hands came all our skills. From his heart came all our loyalty and love.'*

Nessa shuddered. Her every impulse was urging her to get up and walk away. If Farral hadn't been on the point of returning to his own people, she would have. His talk was like the smoke that rose from ambushed villages. It polluted everything it reached.

'He gave us cattle and taught us how to tend them. He gave us fields and taught us how to plough them. He gave us wheat and taught us how to turn it into bread.'

At the moment he said the word 'bread', a half-moon of it dropped into his lap.

They both stared at it, speechless. Just for an instant, Nessa found herself wondering whether it was all true; whether Ogden really did exist and was answering Farral's prayer.

But the bread had not come from his god. It had come from Brockle, who was sitting in the tree above their heads. 'I stole it from an old crow,' she said.

'Good for you,' said Nessa.

It was damp and limp; not the most appetising piece of bread she had ever seen, but it made her mouth water all the same. Farral, however, didn't appear to be having the same reaction. He was examining the bread minutely and, after a moment or two, he looked up into the branches.

'Is it Dog bread?' he asked Brockle. 'I can't tell.'

'Oddly enough,' said Brockle, 'that old crow didn't tell me. For some reason he wasn't in much of a mood for a chat.'

Nessa laughed. All crows were mute. The idea of one talking was ridiculous. But Farral was shaking his head.

'I can't eat it. It could be Cat bread.'

'It's hardly likely,' said Nessa. 'What day is it?'

None of them had the faintest idea.

'Just eat it, Farral,' Nessa went on. 'What harm can it do you? Who's ever going to know?'

Farral didn't answer.

'Do you really think he's watching you?' Nessa managed to spit the despised name from her tongue. 'Ogden? Do you really think he'll condemn you for the rest of your life for eating a piece of bread?'

'All right,' said Farral abruptly. 'I'll eat it. I'll share it with you.'

Nessa stared at him, astonished by the trap she had just walked into; even more astonished by the fact that she had so neatly set it up for herself. She tried to wriggle out. 'But it's bound to be Dog bread, isn't it?' she said. 'I mean, Dogs eat a hundred times more bread than Cats do.'

'So what?' said Farral acerbically. 'What does it matter? Who's ever going to know?'

He tore the bread in two and tossed her a piece. Nessa picked it up and found herself examining it, just as he had. The rain and the trip across the forest had eliminated the distinctions that normally existed between bread cooked in an oven and that cooked on a griddle. There was no way of telling who had made it.

But Farral needed bread. Nessa didn't. She had that one last escape route and was about to try to use it when a nearby sound made her look up. Unheard as they moved among the trees, the grunts had arrived and gathered in a rough semi-circle, watching. They weren't approaching as they usually did. Bonnie, who had by now overcome her mistrust of them and usually engaged in riotous games with the cubs, was also strangely subdued. Nessa knew why. None of them could understand what was happening, but they could all sense the emotional atmosphere. Nessa and Farral had stumbled into a pocket of the ancient enmity that existed between their nations. The grunts, and Bonnie too, could smell it in the air.

Suddenly, the moment was charged with significance. This was more than a petty squabble about a piece of bread. Nessa glanced at Farral. He knew it, too. All that both of them had gone through since they left their villages was being tested; distilled into the decision that hung over her. She could dismiss it all; walk away and never look back. Or she could affirm it; prove that the work she and Farral had done together was of value.

She looked once more at the grunts. Somewhere in their past and her future there was a mystery. She could not say how, but she was certain that it was connected to this brittle moment. And she was just as certain there was only one decision that she could make.

She broke a small corner from the bread. Farral did the same. As they shared the simple food the smell of fear and hatred left the forest air.

Bonnie and the grunts began to play.

2009

Saturday ~~Monday~~: March 9

Klaus is in my shirt pocket, wrapped up in cotton wool. He's OK I'm sure, but a bit shocked. He took a notion to try and gnaw through the wiry web that the Yoke has constructed over the trapdoor. If I had been there I wouldn't have allowed him to try it. He was unconscious for three hours afterwards, poor little thing.

We had another brainstorming session last night, this time to see if we could come up with a way of getting Colin and Oggy out of there. Bernard and Maggie are desperately worried. It's not nice for any of us, but for them it's a form of torture.

We talked about the possibility of tunnelling in and knocking a hole in the wall of the lab, but it didn't get us anywhere. Even assuming we could do it, we would be faced with the same problem. I can't see any of us volunteering to be the first one to stick their nose in and get it zapped by the Yoke. Actually, that's not true. Maggie or Bernard would do it, but they would have to fight off Tina first. She would do anything to make amends and get Oggy and Colin back. It still wouldn't be any use though. The Yoke hasn't given any of us a lethal shock yet, but there's always a first time.

We even discussed the possibility of calling for outside help. We would all, I think, be prepared to jeopardise our existence in Fourth World if that was what it took to save Colin and Oggy. But we couldn't see what even an army could do. They couldn't storm the bunker as if it was a plane. They couldn't bomb the Yoke without bombing the others as well, and there's no telling what it might do if it felt itself under serious threat. All we do know is that it doesn't appear to have any compunction about hurting anyone who gets in its way.

We played with the idea of trying to get hold of some kind of knock-out gas, but in the end we gave up on that as well, since there's no evidence to suggest that the Yoke breathes. The only thing we came up with was another way of trying to starve it out.

The plan was to disconnect the wind- and water-driven turbines up on the hill. That would mean that the batteries down in the bunker wouldn't be recharged when they were emptied. In the meantime, to speed up the draining process, we would turn on every light and every electrical appliance in the house.

We acted on it straight away. Bernard and Danny went off up the mountain to disable the turbines. The rest of us went around the house hunting for things to turn on. There isn't all that much. I turned on the oven and the two rings of a little cooker we use in the summer when the range is out. The freezers were already running. Tina loaded the washing machine and turned it on. Apart from that we could only find a few radios and CD players. Fourth World has no dishwasher, no microwave, no dryer, no vacuum cleaner, no heaters. Sandy dug out an old sewing machine from the attic but when we tried to turn it on it was dead. But she also remembered that there were heaters in the glasshouses, so we took a torch and ran across the orchard and turned them all on full blast.

Our plan didn't come to much. Before midnight we came to see that we had underestimated the Yoke. It had seen Bernard trying to turn off the supply to the lab, and now it must have noticed the drain on the power and worked out what was happening. It beat us at our own game. It turned us off.

So, we have had no power all day, and I'm writing this by candlelight.

Maggie blew a fuse this morning. Not an electrical one, obviously. She just suddenly said she couldn't stand everybody lurking around the house all day and filling it up with doom and gloom. Life had to go on, she told us. There was nothing anybody could do so we might as well keep busy.

She sent Danny and Tina and me off into the woods to cut firewood and although we all set out with long faces I have to admit she was right. We all felt more like ourselves once we got going and started using our bodies again. We met up with Roxy and some of the other talking animals and birds, and we even had a few rusty laughs.

But it was all doom and gloom again when we got back. Colin told us he wasn't feeling too good. Just a bug, he said. Aches and pains and a bit of a headache. He's sure he'll be all right.

I'm sure, too. That's our fish-boy down there. If he can survive being buried in an avalanche for six hours he can sure as hell survive a bit of a cold. Maggie and Bernard don't seem so sure. We keep telling them to stop worrying. We might as well be telling the clouds to stop raining.

2009

Sunday ~~Tuesday~~: March 10

Bernard says the batteries will keep the Yoke going down there for five or six days, depending on how thirsty for juice it is.

It's much too long, especially since Colin's getting worse. He said this morning that he was the same as yesterday except that he felt cold. Colin has never felt cold in his life – his fish genes mean that he's always warm, even when the rest of us are freezing. Bernard told him to get a thermometer from the op. room and take his temperature. He did. It was 103 degrees. Bernard told him where to find the paracetamol – there's a regular pharmacy down there – and he took some of those even though they were out of date. He felt better again after that and he cooked another meal for himself and Oggy. But later in the day he began to deteriorate. He was sitting under the trapdoor talking to Maggie and me, and he began to ramble, making perfect sense one minute then going off at a tangent and talking about some-thing else altogether. Maggie got him to check his temperature again, and there was an awful moment when he said he couldn't read it. He could see the figures but he couldn't make his brain tell him what they meant. He got there eventually and he said his temperature was pretty much normal; just a bit over 98 degrees. But the lapse had put Maggie into a panic. She sent me to fetch Bernard, who was getting a much needed forty winks in the sitting room.

Bernard lost it. He said he was going in there, no matter what that flaming Yoke did to him. He told Colin to stand clear of the door while he went to get the pickaxe, but Colin screamed and pleaded with him not to do it. He said the Yoke was there and was watching and would kill them all. He was so terrified that Bernard had to do what he said. He put the pickaxe down.

He's broken. I can see it. So is Maggie. No matter where you are and what's happening to you there is always something you can do. But when you can hear your own child suffering and you can't do anything to help, something must give way deep down. It has been terrible to watch.

They're fond of me, both of them. I have no doubt about that. They treat me as one of their family, but the truth is I'm not. I was made aware of that today – not by anything they did but by something I did. I left them in the garage and went to get Sandy and Danny to be with their parents and help them any way they could during that awful time.

I went back up to the woods to see if Roxy had any ideas. I thought that since he was a fox he might have some way of approaching the problem that hadn't occurred to us. He said he could dig his way in all right, but he wouldn't be able to get through the wall of the lab so there wasn't much point. He had no other ideas. I stayed there with him until it got dark. It was a miserable wet day and Roxy's fleas kept biting me, but I don't think I ever appreciated the wild, silent world so much in my life. I didn't want to hear what the news was.

I had to, though, when I got back, and it wasn't

good. Colin was slipping further into delirium, making sense less and less often, stringing words together at random. Soon after I got back, Bernard stood up and grabbed the pickaxe again. I thought he was going to have a go at the Yoke's mesh but he grabbed the shovel as well and went out into the dark and the rain. I followed him. He went around the back of the garage. It's a bit of a jungle out there – all brambles and nettles and giant hogweed – but he just barged his way through it all and I barged my way after him. We were both stung and scratched by the time he stopped and started to clear a patch of ground. It was awful to watch – it's amazing what desperation will drive people to do. He was wrenching up thick brambles and briars without a moment's hesitation. He had no gloves and his hands must have been cut to ribbons but he didn't stop until he had two square yards to work in. Then he began to dig.

He picked and I shovelled, then he shovelled and I picked. He was like a demonic machine and I have to admit that I was on my last legs after half an hour or so of that. When Danny came out to see what we were doing I was happy to hand the pick over to him.

The tunnel idea is no more likely to work than it ever was. All the same, I understand why it has to be done. None of us, but particularly Bernard, can do nothing any more.

part
nine

'Have you seen the talking grunts?' said Nessa to Brockle.

'I haven't,' said Brockle, 'but I've met birds who have.' They were on the move again, walking among the trees. High clouds took turns to obscure the sun, but so far it hadn't rained. Brockle was taking a break, perching on Nessa's head. 'I'm not sure I know what the big deal is, really,' she went on.

'Why not?' said Farral.

'I'm sure there is something up there,' she said. 'Whether it's grunts that can talk or some obscure relations of the Cats and Dogs. In any case I doubt they're much different from you lot.'

She was gone before either of them could question her further, whirring through the branches and into the freedom of the wide sky beyond.

'She could be right, you know,' said Farral.

'She usually is,' said Nessa.

The sharing of bread had put new heart into both of them. In doing it, they had taken a step that would have seemed unimaginable to either of them a few weeks ago. Their friendship, just when it appeared to be withering, had found new and deeper ground in which to spread its roots. It would take a very hard storm to damage it now. Nessa had changed her mind about waiting for Farral. If he found a suitable village, she would stay out in the woods while he regained his strength.

But, for the moment at least, it didn't appear to be

necessary. The encounter with the thieving crow had inspired Brockle and Yorick and awakened their parental instincts. They didn't even need to steal from the nearest villages. Most of the Dogs they approached were surprised and charmed to be asked for bread, and gladly gave the birds all they could carry.

The problem was, that wasn't much. Brockle was a big, strong bird and could just about manage to carry a full roti, but half of one was the best that Yorick could manage, and even that proved to be putting too much strain on his damaged wing. Brockle brought Farral six fresh rotis, but it took her all morning and by then the effort was telling on her as well. Farral made her stop for the day. He said he was full and that he felt like a new Dog already, but Nessa knew that six rotis would barely make a snack for a hungry teenager. In the markets she had seen young Dogs eat their way through a dozen rotis in one sitting. It would take more than six a day to build up Farral's strength.

But for now they were moving and for now that was all that mattered. From time to time the sun evaded the clouds and threw twiggy shadows across the forest floor. The birds were fluttering about in the undergrowth, feeding on grubs and berries. There was absolutely nothing to suggest that they were about to walk straight into a disaster.

2009
Wednesday: March 11

The birds had been too enthusiastic about bringing bread for Farral. If it wasn't for that they would have had the usual network of spies out watching for hidden dangers in the forest. The Cats, a small band of guerrillas, were sleeping high up in a stand of close-knit spruce trees. Not even Bonnie, whose nose was always on the alert, could have got scent of them up there.

But their look-out couldn't fail to see Nessa and Farral as they walked directly beneath her, and by some subtle signal that neither of them heard, she succeeded in waking the others. They stayed, as Cats do, completely silent while the little party passed by, but the attention of twenty pairs of eyes, even cleverly veiled, could not escape the blackbird's notice. Yorick saw them and whispered the news to Nessa, then to Farral.

There was no need for discussion. They had been walking uphill for some time and ahead of them the ground continued to rise. One glance, one subtle gesture was all that was needed, and then they were running back the way they had come. Behind them the Cats dropped like rotten fruit from the trees.

Whatever hope they had lay in the decision to go back instead of on. In that initial sprint they were able to get a head start on their pursuers, and as long as the ground continued to slope downwards they might be able to keep their lead. But they both knew they couldn't maintain it for ever. On her own, Nessa might have had some slim chance. With Farral in such a weakened condition they had none.

2009

Thursday: March 12

Neither Nessa nor Farral wasted time in looking back. Yorick informed them about their pursuers, flying beside their ears while he spoke then soaring up to look around again. Each time he descended to their level the news was worse. The Cats were gaining on them. The gentle slope they had been meandering up for half the afternoon was being covered far too fast in reverse. All too soon they would be meeting rising ground again, and then they would be done for.

There was little time for thought, but even so Nessa was vaguely aware of Brockle's absence. She wished the magpie were there with her wise little head. Ideas were in short supply. But help did come, and from the most unexpected quarter. When Nessa first glimpsed the shadowy forms moving through the trees on a parallel run to their own, she thought that the Cats were outflanking them. But as they angled in towards them she could see that they were grunts – their own grunts – some running along with them and others moving at tremendous speed through the branches. The sight gave her heart a faint lift; a momentary warmth in the cold flow of fear. With Yorick's next report the warmth blossomed into hope. The grunts were closing in behind them and haranguing the Cats.

Nessa risked a series of rapid glances over her shoulder. Their pursuers were much closer than she had hoped, spread out in ones and twos; a thin belt of danger behind them. Right the way along the line the grunts were running and swinging and dodging. They made little rushes at the Cats, taking swipes at them, grabbing at their feet or their knees or their clothes, dropping right into their paths from the trees. They weren't stopping the Cats but they were definitely slowing them down. The Cats fended them off with their bows and spears but although they spared no strength in delivering their blows, not one of them resorted to using an arrow or the pointed end of a spear.

Nessa felt a momentary pride in her distant cousins' restraint but there was no time to dwell on it. She returned her attention to the way ahead and to Farral, running alongside her. He was still keeping pace but he wasn't looking good. An uphill stretch would sap his remaining energy in no time. The grunts had bought them precious space but it was still not enough to breathe in.

Beneath their feet the ground levelled off. Yorick advised them to swing to their left, which would allow them to avoid climbing for another half-mile. But already Nessa could see that Farral's strength was giving out. His pace was slowing. One step in every five that he took was a bad one. He was tripping and slipping. He was almost finished.

Her mind moved ahead of her. The Cats wouldn't kill them, she was sure of that. Not immediately anyway. They wouldn't kill her at all, once they got a look at her eyes, but she couldn't say the same for Farral and Bonnie. She could plead for them, of course, and given her status among Cats there was a good chance she could persuade them to spare their lives. What might come after that she couldn't imagine. In any case, she would know all too soon. A fatalism began to creep into her blood but it had no time to spread to her limbs and rob them of strength. Into the confusion a new terror entered, and for Nessa it was the worst one of all.

She felt the sound first, rising up through the earth and vibrating through her bones. She tried to persuade herself that it was her imagination; a waking nightmare where every horror is followed by a worse one. Then she heard it, unmistakably: the thunderous pounding of horses' hooves, heading towards her, growing louder by the moment.

For Nessa it could mean only one thing. For every Cat the sound of galloping hooves was the sound of war. It was passed down from generation to generation, not only in stories but through instinct itself. In peacetime horses moved slowly, pulling ploughs and carts or carrying wealthy merchants. Only in times of war were they gathered together to carry Dog soldiers into battle.

The Cats behind them had the same associations and, along with the grunts, took to the trees immediately. When Yorick informed Farral he dropped to his knees on the ground, unable to think beyond the extreme distress in his body. Even as it happened, Nessa was astonished that her loyalty to a Dog could override one of the most fundamental fears in her being. Against all her instincts she stayed on the ground and went back to Farral. Her heart was outracing his in its terror, but she put her arm round his shoulder and tried to draw him back to his feet. The horses were almost upon them. There was just time for one, dreadful thought.

It was Atticus who had brought this vengeance down upon them. She had eaten Dogs' bread, and she was paying the price.

2009

Wednesday ~~Friday~~: March 13

The Yoke is gone. Yesterday afternoon, while Maggie and Danny were in the garage, it pulled the mesh away from the trap door then burst it open. Maggie and Danny backed off. The Yoke took no notice of them. It came out of the lab, went out through the garage and evaporated. That's what they said, anyway. It got bigger and bigger, like a cloud of smoke, and just drifted away.

We might have been celebrating if it wasn't for Colin. God only knows what it's done to him.

part
ten

Nessa was so convinced that her end had come that it took her several moments to realise, as the horses appeared among the trees, that they were riderless. Even then she didn't understand what was happening until Brockle flew in to land on Farral's head and spelled it out to her. The horses weren't bringing destruction down upon her. They had come to rescue her.

There were about ten of them altogether; a mix of plough horses, hacks and ponies. As they gathered round, snorting and blowing, Nessa backed off, amazed to see that Farral was quite comfortable where he was and didn't appear to have any fear of the enormous hooves that were bruising the ground all around him.

A black pony pursued Nessa. 'Come on, little Cat,' he said. Horses were bad talkers. His voice was strained and nasal; his words barely comprehensible. 'Up you get, up you get.'

Nessa obliged him by climbing swiftly into the nearest tree.

'No time for that, sister,' he said. 'We have to keep moving.'

Nessa looked round and saw why. The guerrillas, realising that there were no Dogs on board the horses, were coming down from the trees again.

Farral was already on his feet. One of the smaller horses, a bright bay cob, was standing beside him, one foreleg bent back at the knee. As Nessa watched, Farral scooped Bonnie up under his arm, stepped onto the uplifted hoof and hopped up on to the cob's back. 'Come on!' he called to Nessa.

The Cats were advancing again. The grunts, slower to overcome their terror of horses, were still in the trees.

'Get on!' said Brockle, hovering at Nessa's ear.

But she couldn't. She had never ridden. Cats didn't. The idea appalled her.

The pony glanced anxiously towards the advancing Cats. 'It's now or never, sister.'

The other horses, Farral's cob among them, were already moving off and gathering speed. Now or never. Nessa took a deep breath and chose now. Grabbing the branch she was on with both hands, she swung herself off it and landed as softly as a falling leaf on the pony's back. She barely had time to grab a handful of his thick mane before she felt his powerful muscles coil and spring as he lit off after his companions. Within moments he was in the midst of them, eating up the ground with long, powerful strides.

If balance were all it took to make a rider, Nessa would have had no problems. But there was far more to it than that. The pony's movements were alien and unpredictable to her. Her body had never learned, as Farral's had, how to flow with them. For her, that headlong dash was a torment of bouncing and sliding and clinging. It was not skill that kept her astride but sheer physical strength.

To make matters worse, staying on was not the only worry she had to contend with. On open ground a Cat is no match for a horse, but in woodland it is different. Undergrowth, broken ground, low or fallen branches – all these things slowed the horses down as much, if not more, than their pursuers. Though they made ground wherever the trees were sparse, there were times when they had to make detours or slow down to pick their way over rocky patches. The birds did their best to find the clearest passages but even they couldn't always find good ground. No matter how wild and furious the pace seemed to Nessa, the guerrillas were never far behind.

But the horses had a plan. They waited until a good stretch of clear ground gave them a bit of an extra lead and then, when they were sure that the Cats had lost sight of them, they split off in pairs and thundered away in five different directions. The Cats, who would be dependent upon their tracks to follow them, would either have to split up into ones and twos or make a choice.

They stayed together. And they followed the wrong pair of horses. Within minutes the birds brought the news. Farral and Nessa were in the clear.

Thursday ~~Saturday~~: March 14

After that awful Sunday night Colin stopped talking altogether. Oggy said he was all right but we were all convinced that he was lying and that Colin was dead.

We had carried on digging around the clock but it isn't as easy as you might think to dig a tunnel. The sides kept collapsing on us, and one time a whole stretch of the tunnel fell in on Danny. It took us about ten minutes to get him out. If it had happened to anyone else they would probably have suffocated or got brain damage, but Danny's dolphin genes saved him. He's capable of holding his breath underwater for seven or eight minutes. The last bit was scary, he said, but he managed to hold on.

I suppose if we'd had more time or if we'd given it a bit more thought, we might have come up with a better system, but the truth is that none of us were thinking straight, least of all Bernard. There was just this awful, frantic energy. I hope I never have to go through anything like that again. Every day seemed to take for ever and then, just when we were finally getting somewhere with our tunnel, it was suddenly all over.

The next day, the Monday, we realised that Oggy wasn't lying. Colin was alive, we knew that. But I couldn't write anything. I don't even want to try and describe the kind of sounds he was making. I don't even want to remember them. What has happened to him still makes my blood run cold. Physically he's fine – he has loads of energy and a great appetite. He was delighted to see us yesterday when the yoke left and we went down into the bunker. The trouble is he can't talk and he can't understand anything that's said to him.

Maggie and Bernard are holding on to the hope that he still hasn't recovered from whatever bug he had. They talk about temporary amnesia a lot and keep prompting him with significant words and talking about things that have happened. Nothing seems to register. He babbles and warbles and the odd recognisable word sometimes get mixed up in his gibberish, but it's obvious he doesn't know what he's saying. Maggie and Bernard say it's a symptom of the illness but I don't think it is. Nor does Danny. We talked about it this morning. We think it's the result of it.

When they were sure they had shaken off the Cats that day they hid out in a safer part of the forest. The pony told them his name was Bob; he had been the finest of friends with his young Dog rider until he had been asked to carry him on manoeuvres in a training camp. The cob, whose name was Ginny, said little. Whatever her experiences had been they seemed to cause her great pain, and she politely declined to speak about them. For their part, Nessa and Farral withheld nothing. They told the horses the story of their strange friendship, their reasons for being there, that they were on a search for talking grunts. The horses were fascinated, asking question after question, clearly delighted to find a Cat and a Dog who were as appalled by the escalating conflict as they were. At nightfall they went off in search of their scattered friends, but in the morning they were there again, and they offered to go along with them, into the Foul Land and beyond.

The arrival of the horses into their lives provided Nessa and Farral with more than a miraculous escape. Although neither of them had thought of it, horses provided the obvious answer to their biggest problem. Now Farral could ride instead of walking. With a bit of bread from Brockle and the more digestible bits of Nessa's catch he was certain that he would be able to carry on. Nessa wasn't so confident about his strength, but she realised that they had to get as far away from that area as possible. Now that the word of their unusual presence would be spreading, there would be eyes and ears everywhere.

For a few days Nessa was in all kinds of pain. She was stiff and bruised from that first, wild ride and neither riding nor walking was comfortable. But as time went on the aches and pains wore off and, at the more reasonable pace of their regular travel, she learned all she needed to know about riding a talking horse. The only regret that Nessa had about the horses was that they had put their new-found friends off their trail. It saddened her, and Farral too, to think that they might never see the grunts again.

Friday ~~Sunday~~: March 15

I spent almost the whole day observing Colin and trying to look as if I wasn't. It's an awful thing to admit to, but there's something about the way he behaves that is absolutely fascinating.

I hate to say it, but I think that when we first saw him in the lab we closed our minds to him, as though he wasn't really Colin any more. He frightened us. He was dirty and hungry. He couldn't talk to us. He had wet himself and worse. He smelled bad. But now that he's all cleaned up and comfortable we can see – or I can, anyway – that he is still Colin. And as time goes on we are getting a better idea about his condition.

The first thing we realised is that he hasn't lost his memory, or not all of it, anyway. He knows his way around the house and gardens. He knows where his bedroom is and took himself off there last night and tonight. This morning he went racing off to the orchard. I followed him and found him rooting around under the trees. All the apples were brought in during the autumn; he obviously doesn't remember that, but he does remember they were there once. When he didn't find them he ran back to the house and out into the shed where the apples are stored. He picked an eater, not a cooker, even though the eaters are all tiny and wrinkly and scabby and the cookers are still plump and green. So all that kind of stuff is still in his head, but he can't manage other, basic things like using a spoon or turning a door handle.

Maggie had put him in a nappy because of the mess he was in when we found him in the lab, but Tina worked out this morning that he doesn't need it. He knows when he needs the bathroom and he knows how to get there. The only bit he can't manage is his clothes, so someone has to help him. He's fine with that too. He's not the least bit embarrassed.

In fact, it's noticeable that he is remarkably contented in almost every way. Before the illness he was somehow too serious for a ten-year-old. He was always thinking; always worrying about something or other. I hardly ever heard him laugh. I wouldn't dare say it to Bernard or Maggie, but in a weird sort of way he seems happier. He spent ages this afternoon romping around with Loki and afterwards he came in and got fascinated by the pups. He touched their noses and poked their fat tummies and he even picked one of them up and carried it around for a while. He didn't cuddle it and stroke it the way he would have done before. He just carried it, then put it down on top of the fridge when he got interested in something else.

I keep trying to put my finger on what it is that has changed in him. There has been quiet mention of brain damage and maybe that's what it is. But I have this nagging feeling in the back of my mind. There is something about his condition that is familiar. His pattern of behaviour isn't random. It's one that I recognise. It isn't that he doesn't have intelligence. It's just a different kind of intelligence. More like

It's 6 a.m. I must have sat and stared at the wall for two hours after I wrote that last bit. My mind is scaring me stiff, putting more and more bits of this terrible jigsaw together. The way my thoughts were going led me to another big question and I just had to go down to the lab to find the answer, even though it was even scarier down there. Oggy was the only one awake in the house and, fair dues to him, he came down with me. The way my theory is shaping up depended upon what was on the computer. Or, more specifically, what wasn't on it. I've been down there now for three hours, going through every last one of Bernard's and Maggie's files, aware the whole time of the creepy creature that had last done the same thing.

I didn't find what I was looking for. I knew I wouldn't. There was no way Maggie and Bernard were going to leave evidence of their experiments sitting around for some hacker to find, or some nosy cop or soldier who might come poking around. Even that first article that Bernard wrote – the one that was rubbished by the rest of the scientific community and brought him to Maggie's attention – that isn't there either.

I wish I had found them. I wanted to find them. I used every search facility on the computer but they just aren't there. If they had been they would have turned my thoughts away from the terrible direction they're taking. I don't care now who laughs at my theory. I hope they laugh. I hope they prove it's all crazy pie in the sky. My worst fear is that they won't. Because there was something else I was looking for down in the lab and I didn't find that, either.

The yeti's stone.

There were pheasants again in the lowlands and pigeons and goats and hares in the hills. There were grunts, too, but none that they knew.

Yorick took on the job of look-out, which left Brockle free to fetch bread for Farral and to scout on ahead to assess the best route. When Nessa asked her one morning why she stayed with them she replied that she had never been so happy in her life. She enjoyed rearing chicks, she said, and she loved educating them right up until they were able to be independent, but that only took up part of each year. The rest of the time she didn't know what to do with herself. Other birds thought she was a gossip and a busybody, but she wasn't. She just had more mental energy than she knew what to do with.

On horseback, they covered twice the amount of ground in a day than they had on foot. The horses thought nothing of travelling from dawn to dusk, and often well beyond. At night they poached grass from the farmland at the edges of the forest, or searched out wild meadows in the hills. A few hours' sleep seemed to be all they needed and even that they took standing up.

They were good companions and, despite their obvious reservations, they never faltered in their determination to stay with Nessa and Farral. The most dangerous moments came when their way led them across a river. The only way to get to the other side was by a rickety wooden bridge. A

Dog village stood on the nearest bank. There was no alternative but to pass through it and hope for the best. They went by night, galloped through the village and straight over the bridge. By the time the Dogs woke and rallied, they were long gone. But Ginny said afterwards that she had never been more terrified in her life. Going through the village was one thing. Crossing that flimsy bridge at full speed, with the boards rattling and the black water slithering along underneath had almost been too much for her.

So when they arrived, one early morning soon afterwards, at the high wall that marked the edge of the Foul Land, Nessa expected that Ginny, and probably Bob as well, would let them go on alone.

'We'll never get over that,' said Bob.

'No,' said Ginny. 'Not a chance.'

All four of them stood and stared at it gloomily for several minutes. Then Bob said. 'There's only one thing for it. You're going to have to pull it down.'

2009

Saturday ~~Monday~~: March 16

We've all down in the bunker. The trapdoor has been made airtight and beyond that we've sealed up the garage doors and windows as well as we can. I haven't slept for more than thirty-six hours and we've all been chasing round like lunatics for the past few of them, making sure that everything we'll need for the foreseeable future is down here with us. Danny was out fishing for a lot of the day and I have been fetching and carrying for him, up and down the glen. My legs feel like two broken fenceposts but the freezer is packed to the gunnels with fish. We've got a mountain of spuds (more fetching and carrying from the village shop), a ton of oats and a ton of wheat (plus grinder), a sack each of onions, carrots and swedes, a few cheeses and a few boxes of sad-looking apples. It seems like loads, but the fact is that there's no way of telling. And there's one other necessity that we might run out of. Air. We have a fall-back plan to deal with that. It could be very risky and none of us much likes it, but it was the best we could come up with.

I think we've all been swinging between two wild extremes all day. Panic at one end and a sense of absurdity at the other. I hope it's all for nothing and we'll emerge feeling foolish to find that nothing has changed. The trouble is that we have no idea how long we're going to have to stay here before we find out.

I'm completely wrecked. The bunks never did get made, but we brought down mattresses and bedding and even hot-water bottles. I'm going to be the first to try them out.

'*Between the death of the old world and the birth of the new, the father of all Cats was born. His name was Atticus.*'

The night air was cold but there was no rain in it. Nessa and Farral were sitting opposite each other on a wooded mountainside. Between them was the first fire they had lit since they began their journey together. On a spit of green hazel two haunches of kid were roasting.

'*For twenty years he stayed in the ocean, waiting while the new world prepared itself for his reign. When he was ready, he stepped out on to the land. He could see in the dark and hunt down anything that lived and breathed.*'

Farral glanced into the darkness behind him, first over one shoulder and then over the other. The Foul Land was no place to hear words like that. If Nessa noticed, or shared his disquiet, she gave no sign of it.

'*The crawling Cats spread the word among all the gifted creatures on earth that their god had come to walk among them.*'

Nessa paused, leaned forward and turned the meat. They had deliberated long and hard before agreeing to light the fire. The place they were in was bleak and cold, the land acid, the soil black and heavy. They were three days into the Foul Land already and the birds had not seen hide nor hair of Cat nor Dog. Despite the certainty of the birds and animals that this edge of the Foul Land was quite safe, there were no villages north of the wall. If it was now a fit place to live in, neither community had yet discovered it. It made their travelling easier, but it also meant that there was no more bread for Farral. He needed cooked meat.

'But the Dogs and the hounds were jealous of his power,' Nessa went on. *'They conspired against him and his followers and there were battles between the hounds and the crawling Cats. He took up home in the forests which are the true home of the Cat.'*

Nessa fell quiet, alerted by a sound beyond the circle of the firelight. Bonnie went to investigate, and Nessa and Farral heard a quiet conversation taking place beneath the trees. They got up to follow Bonnie but she was already on her way back.

'Goat,' she said.

'Goat?' said Nessa and Farral together.

'She wasn't too happy about your dinner there. She said to watch out. Most of the goats around here are gifted.'

'The goats are?' said Farral. 'I never heard of a gifted goat.'

'Nor me,' said Bonnie. 'But I just met one.'

Nessa looked at the meat above the fire. 'That wasn't one, anyway. At least, I'm pretty sure it wasn't.'

Bonnie returned to her share of the kid, which she had chosen to eat raw. Farral turned the spit and Nessa sat back down. After a while she began to talk again. *'From the old world he took a wife, that he might bring children into the new world. To those children he gave the Cat law.'*

She looked into the flames. Farral prompted her. 'What is the Cat law, Nessa?'

She looked across the fire at him, then back into the flames.

'The mute beasts give up their flesh for him.
The gifted beasts he honours. The trees he protects.
If his enemy oppresses him, let him call on me.
And remember that the new world and all things in it
Belong to the Cat.'

When she had finished, Farral waited for a moment and then, as though in answer, said,

'The old world is dead. The new world lies at your feet.
Its stones are for your farms. Its game is for your table.
If enemies confront you, stand tall. Sharpen your teeth.
The sons and daughters of Ogden have inherited the earth.
Let none dispute it.'

The spit burned through abruptly and the meat dropped
on to the fire, sending up a burst of sparks. Nessa and Farral
lunged forward, rescued a haunch each and dragged them
clear. Farral sliced the outermost layer from his, then cut
a new spit and returned the rest to roast. Nessa left hers
on a stone to cool a little. She gave Bonnie a warning
glance.

'Do you know the Song of Atticus?' she said to Farral.

Farral's mouth was full. He shook his head.

Nessa spoke the words:

'I am the eye of the night,
The unwavering watch,
The tight spring.

I am the listening dark.
I hear the moonvoice
Teaching the wind
How to sing

As I dance the deathdance
With every warm
And trembling thing.

I am the beast and the beauty.

The unfettered heart
Has no heartstring.'

Farral stopped chewing. A noise behind him made him swing round and grab for the handle of his knife, but it was only Bob and Ginny, returning from their grazing expedition.

He turned back to Nessa. She was tearing into the haunch of kid with her teeth, unaware of the effect the poem had had upon him. As he watched her, he understood for the first time how powerful an influence her culture must have had upon her, and how far she had come in accepting him as a friend.

Sunday ~~Tuesday~~: March 17

Yesterday began for me before the day before had finished. There was no way I could sleep with all that stuff going on in my head. I just had to get it off my chest.

I made mint tea for Maggie and Bernard and took it to their room. It felt wrong to be waking them. I knew how badly they needed sleep after all that had happened. But if there was any chance at all that I was right, it had to be done.

'Is it my birthday?' said Bernard, and fell instantly back to sleep.

'Where's Colin?' said Maggie, before she even opened her eyes.

'In his room.' I had checked as I passed by. He was still sleeping.

She heaved herself up into a sitting position but she didn't look comfortable. She never looks comfortable these days. I handed her the tea and wished I had something better to offer. Rashers and eggs and sausages I used to bring my mum, back in the old days. Orange juice. Forgotten pleasures.

Maggie took a sip of her tea and put it on the bedside table. 'What's all this in aid of, Christie?'

'I've got thoughts I wanted to run by you. Before the others get up.'

Maggie shook Bernard by the shoulder. He moaned,

then growled, and finally sat up. He didn't look too happy. I wondered if it was all such a good idea after all. His first sip of tea burned his lip.

'Definitely not my birthday,' he said irritably. Maggie put a hand over his.

I've got a theory about the Yoke,' I said. 'I want you to shoot it down.'

'Consider it done,' said Bernard, and would have snuggled down under the covers again if Maggie hadn't stopped him.

Let's hear it,' she said.

It still wasn't easy. I didn't know where to start. 'If you were the Yoke,' I said, 'and you crash-landed on earth, what would you do?'

Bernard's tone was heavy with sarcasm. 'I don't know, Christie. What would I do?'

Maggie reproached him and he apologised to me, but he had stopped me in my tracks. I tried another angle.

'You know when we went to Tibet to look for clues about how the missing link gene got into the human race? Well, I think we might have found one after all. We just didn't realise it at the time.'

That was a better approach, all right. Bernard was suddenly interested. 'Go on.'

'Ok. Well, say the Yoke crash-landed here. I don't know how or why. It doesn't matter. What we have is this sophisticated life form and it finds itself on a planet with no intelligent life. It can't get home. It can't send a message or anything to let the other Yokes know where it is. It's stuck.'

'I don't get you,' said Maggie. 'There is intelligent life here.'

'There is now,' I said. 'But there wasn't when the Yoke landed here.'

'How long ago are you talking about?' said Bernard.

'I don't know exactly,' I said. 'Before early man was around, anyway. Let's say a million years.'

'Oh, come on,' said Bernard. 'You're not trying to tell me that thing has been hanging around here for a million years?'

'At least,' I said.

'So how come it waited until now to pay us a visit?'

'It had to,' I said. 'And in any case, it didn't decide to pay us a visit. We brought it here.'

It sounded so mad that they had to listen.

'Put yourself in the Yoke's shoes,' I said. 'You're here on this planet, a million or more years ago. You have no way of phoning home. We know something about what the Yoke can do. It's amazingly clever, but it's not clever enough to build a radio telescope out of mud and stones. Even where the Yoke comes from that requires an advanced level of civilisation. Factories. Industries. Some efficient form of energy. On its own it just can't do it.

'So it has to figure out another way. It has two things on its side. One of them is time. I think it operates under completely different laws from us.'

'Patently,' said Bernard sourly.

'Shh,' said Maggie.

'The other one . . .' I dried up for a minute. This was where it got really difficult. 'The other one is its genes. It's a genetic engineer. It's a little self-contained biochemistry lab.'

Bernard sighed. 'A lab.'

I knew I'd lost him but I had to keep going. 'If I'm right we're all in terrible danger. The whole planet is.'

Now Maggie sighed. 'Christie,' she said, 'we're all upset about what has happened to Colin. We might not be saying it but I suspect we're all a bit nervous that the bug might be contagious. There's nothing we can do about that except keep our fingers crossed.'

'It's not contagious,' I said. 'Not yet, anyway.'

'All the same, there's no sense in letting our imaginations run away with us, is there?'

I shook my head in agreement. That was exactly the kind of thing I wanted to hear. But I had to tell it all. There was more of it that I wanted to have rubbished. 'I think the Yoke put the missing link gene into the apes. Then it went to sleep and waited for evolution to happen. You know the way it can change its density? You saw it, Maggie, when it floated away.'

She nodded. I could see that she was just humouring me now.

'Well, if it can make itself less dense, what's to stop it making itself more dense? If you could make yourself into practically anything and you had to wait around for a few millennia, what would you turn yourself into?'

'I don't know,' said Maggie. She was trying to hide an indulgent little smile. 'What?'

'I think we brought the Yoke back from Tibet. Or I did. I think it's the yeti's stone.'

Maggie let the little smile come out, but to my surprise I found I had Bernard's interest back again. I knew it by the way he was looking at me. I could see his mind revving up behind his eyes.

'He might have something there,' he said to Maggie. 'It gave me the same kind of shock, after all. And we haven't seen the stone since the Yoke appeared.'

'It's not there now,' I said. 'I've just searched the whole lab complex from top to bottom.'

'This morning?' said Maggie. It still wasn't light, and it wouldn't be for quite some time. 'How long have you been up?'

'All night. I couldn't sleep.'

'This is really bothering you, isn't it, Christie?' said Bernard. There was a new tone in his voice, one that I didn't hear very often. He was genuinely concerned about me. It made my tear ducts sting. He was right. I was in an awful state.

'I'm not sure how far I can go along with your theory,' he said, 'but you might be on to something with this stone business. Why Tibet, though?'

I cleared my throat. The tears had stayed put. 'That was just a coincidence,' I said. 'And a pretty weird one, as it happens. We know from the story the yeti told us that they were the original model. They were the species that we evolved from.'

'That's right,' said Bernard.

'The stone was precious to the yeti. If I'm right, it had been in the keeping of her ancestors for thousands of generations. But, ironically, they were the ones who evolved the least because our lot drove them up into the mountains. They never created the kind of civilisation that the Yoke was waiting for — they couldn't — and there was no way that the Yoke could know it was all happening somewhere else on the planet.'

'So if we hadn't gone poking around it might still have been there?'

'It might have been there for ever,' I said.

'And it might not,' said Maggie. 'It might have woken up when it realised all the yetis were dead and gone for a little look around.'

'Do you believe it, then?' I said.

Bernard blew breath up his face and made his fringe stand up. Maggie didn't answer the question. She asked another one instead.

'What makes you think we're in danger?'

Before I could reply we got interrupted by Tina

coming in with an armload of Electra's kittens. They are still tiny little things – furry puddings with legs that stick out at the sides – but they've already coming out with their first words. They say 'Mum' and 'milk' ('meeook') and 'Tina'. We tried to get them on to 'Dad' and 'light' and 'Christie', but Electra had been out most of the night and they were pretty much fixated on 'Mum' and 'milk'. Tina took them off to find both and I didn't waste any time before launching back into my theory. If Colin woke up it could be a long time before I got their attention back.

'I think the Yoke made the virus that Colin got,' I said. 'And I think I know why.'

part
eleven

Over the days that followed the horses carried Nessa and Farral across an ever-changing landscape. There were windswept hills where no trees could grow, dense, tangled woods of spruce and rhododendron, and places where the hills and forests gave way to great tracts of dangerous bogland which made them take long detours. On the sixth day they came to the ruins of a great city on the sea, so big that they were picking their way through its jumbled and over-grown ruins from dawn to dusk.

'They must have been giants, the people of the old world,' said Farral, as they circumvented a leaning slab of mossy stone the breadth of a full-grown tree and the height of five. 'A whole village and all their horses couldn't lift a stone like that.'

The winds were fierce and cold, and occasionally brought icy rain. The Foul Land gave them all bad dreams, but they didn't see any of the terrors that were reputed to live there. They saw no grunts either but there were more gifted creatures than Nessa and Farral had ever encountered. Goats watched closely from the ridges as they passed, but kept well clear of Nessa's hunting range. One afternoon she sprang from Bob's back to grab a mesmerised mouse and was astonished to hear it plead, in a tiny high voice, for its life. In the woods, squirrels called out to them as they passed and dropped spruce-cones on their heads. Badgers approached their damp, smouldering camp fires and asked them what their business was.

But, as always, the birds were the first and the best sources of information. Yorick and Brockle were amazed by the number who could talk. The further north they went the higher the proportion grew, until the gifted birds began to outnumber the mute ones.

Beyond the ancient city the Foul Land was known by a different name. The birds and animals referred to it as the Deadlands, but they agreed with Brockle's southern informants in all other respects. It had caused dreadful illnesses and deaths in the past, unspeakable horrors had lived there and perhaps still did, but its eastern reaches at least were quite safe now. There was no wall on the northern side of it and by the time they realised that, they had already passed out of it and into the world that they had been told did not exist. It was cold and wet. The hills were high and the skies were low, and each of them was as dark and forbidding as the other. But it was a real land, with trees and rivers and birds and animals. No villages. Not yet.

Yorick and Brockle began to report some confused answers to their questions. Some of the birds, particularly the younger ones, had no idea what grunts were. They said they'd never seen them, gifted or otherwise. When they had grunts described to them, they asserted that they were people, and all of them said there were plenty of them a bit further north. When asked whether the people were Cats or Dogs, the local birds became even more perplexed. Some of them flew off in alarm. Others took pains to explain that cats and dogs had four legs and people only had two.

'How can they be people if they're not Cats or Dogs?' said Nessa.

Farral didn't know, either. But other birds, older or better-travelled, understood what Yorick and Brockle were asking of them. They knew about Dogs, Cats and talking grunts. Without exception they confirmed that the travellers were heading in the right direction.

2009

Monday ~~Wednesday~~: March 18

I got writer's cramp there yesterday. Today's almost gone but I have to finish the story.

I had Maggie and Bernard's attention after telling them that I thought the Yoke created the virus. They were riveted by that.

'You always said that the missing link gene came out of nowhere,' I said to Bernard. 'You even wrote about it, the way it has a different structure to all the other genes we have. So if I'm right and the Yoke introduced it into the ape, or the yeti, it means it has the capacity to do genetic engineering on other species without the need of any kind of extra equipment.'

'Your "walking lab" theory.'

'Right.'

'It's not beyond the bounds of possibility,' said Bernard. 'Nothing is where that creature is concerned. It can obviously do some pretty amazing things.'

'Yes. So, remember that Colin said the Yoke pricked him? When he first got locked into the bunker?'

Maggie nodded, uncomfortable with the memory.

'Well, he said it was like a needle, didn't he? I think the Yoke made a needle out of itself the way it made an electric plug. To take a sample of Colin's blood. So it could make the virus.'

'It's all possible, I suppose,' said Bernard. 'But why?'

The next bit was going to be difficult. I took a deep breath. 'I think I know why the virus made Colin the way he is. I think it rampaged through every cell of his body and wiped out the missing link gene.'

It was, understandably, more than either of them could take on board. Maggie reacted by getting up and going to the bathroom. Afterwards I heard her heavy steps going along the landing towards Colin's room. The notion that their child could be used as a guinea pig was bad enough. That the result of the experiment might have permanently deprived him of the capacity for reason was unbearable.

Bernard's reaction was, predictably, to pour scorn on the theory. 'That's ridiculous, Christie. You're raving. Do something useful, will you? Stop thinking and put the porridge on.'

Breakfast was a dreadful affair. Bernard brooded and snapped at everyone who opened their mouth. Maggie occupied herself with Colin, who was a disaster area with the porridge. He couldn't use a spoon and he wouldn't consent to being fed with one, either. He wanted to eat the porridge with his fingers, but every time he dipped them in the bowl he burned them and yelled. But he didn't get angry the way a frustrated toddler would. He behaved more like a dog might, or a cat, given a hot sausage. He paced backwards and forwards, approached the delicious but dangerous bowl from different angles, sniffed at it and gave it the occasional tentative prod. I thought Maggie should have left him alone to work it out for himself but she couldn't stand it. She took the porridge away and made him some fresh rotis instead, which he ate with great pleasure.

After breakfast was finished I offered to take him with me to collect some of the firewood we had cut the week before. We haven't seen our talking pony since the day the armed gang came so we have no one to pull the cart and we have to hump all the wood down on our backs, or in the wheelbarrow. It's heavy, boring work, and having Colin along would have been no hardship even if he wasn't any help. He would have enjoyed it in any case. But Bernard said he wanted to talk, so he went up with me instead.

I thought he was going to tick me off for upsetting Maggie, but that wasn't it. We were barely out of earshot of the house when he started to grill me.

'If this virus of yours really exists, how did the Yoke transmit it to Colin?' he said.

'The sneeze,' I said. 'Remember the sneeze? An expulsion of little droplets into the air.'

He nodded. From his expression, I figured he'd already thought of that himself and it had led him to his next question. 'So if it attacks the missing link gene, why didn't Oggy get it?'

We were walking along the edge of the glen towards the spruce woods, taking it in turns to push the wheelbarrow. Hushy and Darling and one of the blackbirds, Ackerbill, were playing chicken games with Loki, who was getting her first proper walk since the pups were born.

'Oggy didn't get it because you covered your tracks so well,' I said.

'You what?'

'You left nothing on the computer about putting the missing link gene into animals. No one else in the world knows about it. It's not written up anywhere. There's no way the Yoke could know.'

'But Oggy was right under its nose!'

'So what? It can't hear – we figured that out already. If it can't hear it may have no concept of speech. It saw a domesticated quadruped, that's all. It even looked it up to be on the safe side – Oggy told us it was reading about dogs on the Internet.'

'All right, all right,' he said irritably. 'Maybe that's possible. But why on earth would it want to eliminate the missing link? After it went to all the trouble to put it there?'

That was the one thing I was really wobbly on. 'I don't know. It's served its purpose, I suppose. And maybe now it just wants to tidy up after itself. Leave the place as it found it.

Bernard snorted, a kind of failed attempt at a laugh. 'You'll have to do better than that.'

'I can't,' I said. 'But in a way it doesn't matter. If it wipes us all out it doesn't help us much to know why, does it?'

'Wipes us all out?'

'That's what it's planning to do, Bernard. That's what I think, anyway. All those maps of the globe and all that stuff about weather systems. The virus is carried by air and moisture. It's going to rain it down on the whole planet.'

Bernard sighed. 'Christie . . . can you hear what you're saying? I know the Yoke frightened us all, but this is totally far-fetched.'

'Why did it seal up the trap door, then?' I asked him. The mesh. The airtight seal. Why would it do that?'

'Now you've defeating your own argument,' said Bernard. 'If your theory about the virus holds water it wants it to spread. It doesn't want to prevent it from spreading.'

'It wants it to spread, but not yet. It needs us for a bit longer. It needs the power stations to keep running until it can get to a transmitter and send its message. Then it can do what it likes with us.'

We walked on in silence while Bernard chewed that over. To my alarm he wasn't doing a great job of shooting down my theory. I wished he would get on with it. Eventually he said, 'Surely to God it must be impossible to spread a virus over a whole planet? It couldn't be done.'

I couldn't imagine the mechanics of it either, but it didn't follow for me that it couldn't be done. 'Plugging yourself into the mains supply can't be done either,' I said. 'Nor can turning yourself into a cloud.'

Bernard said nothing more until we reached the woodpile. He started to fill the wheelbarrow, then stopped. 'There's one way to find out,' he said.

'Find out what?'

'If you're right. About Colin's bug.'

Of course there was. I was amazed that I hadn't thought of it myself. The lab had been designed to find and isolate genetic material. It would be a relatively simple project for either Maggie or Bernard to test Colin's DNA and find out if the missing link gene was there or not.

The sense of relief that came over me was indescribable. I felt as though the whole weight of the problem had been shifted from my shoulders. More than that, I was suddenly convinced that none of it was real. The gene would be found. Colin would recover. The Yoke was gone for good. We would all live happily ever after.

But Bernard appeared to be having an equal and opposite reaction. As I grew calmer and happier, he grew increasingly agitated until, finally, he threw down the sticks he was gathering and yelled to the skies, 'Darling!'

She arrived within seconds.

'Go back to the house!' he said to her. 'Tell Maggie and the others to start packing everything they need for a month in the bunker. Now!'

Darling took off like an arrow, and a second later we were both running after her, hell for leather along the path to Fourth World.

'They're Dogs!' said Nessa, unable to keep the disgust and disappointment out of her voice.

'They can't be,' said Farral, but he had to admit that it appeared as if she was right.

They were looking down into a long, broad valley. Parts of it were wooded, other parts cultivated in neat fields and terraces. Beneath them was a small village centred around a communal well. Smoke rose from several of the chimneys. Spread out along the valley, in both directions, were more, similar settlements. At the mouth of the valley, far away to the east, they could just make out the smooth grey shine of the sea.

Behind them, just below the ridge, the horses were grazing hungrily. They had started before dawn and, guided by an excitable young starling, had travelled without a break throughout the day.

'Well, sister?' said Ginny. 'You find your pot of gold?'

'I'm still looking for the rainbow,' said Nessa. 'They're just Dogs.'

Brockle had been scouting around down below. She heard what Nessa said as she returned to them. 'If they're Dogs,' she said, 'why don't they call themselves Dogs?'

'Maybe they don't know they're Dogs,' said Nessa disdainfully. 'But that's what they are.'

In the village below something was happening. People were emerging from their houses, one by one, and were gathering beside the well. They were too far away for Nessa to see them clearly, but not too far away for her to see which way they were looking. Every face was turned towards the ridge where she and Farral were standing. She ducked down and pulled Farral with her.

'That starling! She's gone and ratted on us!'

Yorick and Brockle lifted off and floated down the steep side of the valley. Nessa raised her head and watched them. The villagers were already moving between the houses, heading in their direction. Two yellow hounds detached themselves from the group and took the lead.

'They're coming,' said Nessa. 'Let's go!'

'No,' said Farral. 'Let's wait.'

'You wait if you like,' said Nessa. 'They're obviously your people, after all.'

She ran across to Bob and sprang onto his back. He didn't move.

'Come on, Bob,' she hissed at him. 'You've got to get me out of here.'

'Nessa,' Farral called. 'They've stopped.'

Nessa slipped down again and crawled back to the ridge on her hands and knees. The advance party had indeed stopped and had gathered into a group again, on the hillside above the village. Despite the fact that all her nerves were itching to be gone, Nessa stayed where she was and waited. Apart from the rush of the wind and the busy cropping of the horses, there was no sound at all. Minute by minute the light was fading and it was getting increasingly difficult to see what was happening down below. When Yorick and Brockle returned they seemed to pop out of the gloom as though it had just given birth to them.

'They're not Dogs,' said Yorick breathlessly.

'How do you know?' said Nessa.

'Brockle asked them,' he said, with barely concealed admiration. 'I would never have thought of it.'

'What are they, then?'

'People,' said Brockle.

'What's that supposed to mean?' said Nessa. 'That's like saying you're a bird. What kind of people are they, that's what we want to know.'

'No kind of people,' said Brockle. 'Just people. Talking grunts, if you like. But they want to meet you. They're really excited that you've come. I told them not to come and get you. I told them that I'd bring you down.'

'There's no way I'm going down there,' said Nessa.

'You can trust them,' said Brockle. 'I'm sure you can.'

'*You* can trust them, Brockle. You're not a Cat.'

Farral had said nothing until now. He had listened to all that was said, staring down into the darkness that had descended upon the valley. When he spoke, there was a quiet certainty in his voice. 'We have to go, Nessa.'

'Why?'

'Because there's nothing else for us to do. I don't know who or what these people are, but they're the reason we came here. We can't turn round without seeing this through to the end.'

Nessa followed his gaze towards the valley, where lights were flickering into life, one by one.

'You know he's right, Nessa,' said Yorick.

2009

Tuesday ~~Thursday~~: March 19

Darling is down here with us, but we didn't bring any of the other birds or animals. They're not in the same danger that we are, and we can't afford to share the resources.

It was awful leaving them behind. Oggy has promised to look after Loki and the pups. I know he can do it. I've seen him kill a sheep and this time he has the Dobermen to help him if he needs them. Loki will be fine. I just wish I didn't miss her so much. I wish she hadn't tried so hard to be brave.

The cats will be fine as well. Electra is a great huntress and Oedipus is a top-class thief. The rest of the talking animals are pretty much independent anyway. Maggie and Bernard had their heads screwed on in that respect. It would have been easy to make cutesy, cuddly pets out of some of the woodland folk, but they didn't do it. They're the luckiest ones now. The farm animals are the biggest worry. Sandy turned them all out to range across the land and take their chances. I sent Hushy with a message to Roxy to keep a protective eye on the hens, but other than that there was nothing more we could do for them.

Bernard is doing tests on Colin's blood. We all thought it was going to be a nightmare taking blood from him, but he surprised us. He yelped and made a ferocious face, and tried to pull his arm away. But the minute it was over he completely forgot about it and went bouncing around in his usual, light-hearted way.

I really hope I'm wrong. There's plenty of room down here for the seven of us but it still feels horribly claustrophobic. We're used to spending half our lives out in the open air and using a lot of energy. Poor old Danny's finding it particularly hard. He misses the sea and there isn't even a bath down here that he can lie in. We have to take turns washing in a big plastic storage box. We're all assuming that the water's safe because it comes from a spring deep underground, but we can't really be sure. Just have to hope for the best.

Everyone has heard my theory now and no one has been able to pick any significant holes in it. One positive thing that has emerged is that it has made Tina feel a bit better. If I'm right, then her attempt to shoot the yoke was irrelevant. It just happened that it was ready, at that moment, to try out the virus. If she and Colin hadn't come down here that night it would have seized on the first person it saw in the morning.

No one pursued that line of thought. None of us would choose to be in Colin's shoes.

Although, in fact, we wouldn't be. He doesn't wear any. He can't get his clothes off, though he pulls and drags at them sometimes, but he can get his shoes off and he does. For a while Maggie spent half her time following him around and struggling with him to get them back on. It was really important to her. She didn't spell it out, but I suppose her thinking was that if he was properly dressed he could still be regarded as

As what? I didn't mean to go there. Of course he's human. He's Colin. And in some ways he's doing better than any of us. He never gets bored. He wears us all out, tearing around the place and playing with us all. He loves chasing games and he's into any kind of rough and tumble stuff that we're willing to join in, but he knows his own strength – he bites and kicks and grabs but he always stops just short of hurting anyone. When he gets tired he snuggles up to Maggie or Bernard or Sandy, or he just goes off to the bunk room and falls asleep.

And even though he doesn't reason or speak we can tell that he remembers certain things about his environment. He never goes anywhere near anything electrical apart from the computer, which he sometimes sits and watches as though he expects some kind of response from it. He can't turn on the tap but he knows that water comes from it. If he wants something he can't have, like a piece of cheese or an apple, he doesn't get hung up on it – he just goes off and does something else. He can be a bit wearing sometimes, like when he has bags of energy and no one else has, but most of the time he's a pleasure to be around.

The worst thing of all is that he's so funny. We were all too shocked in the beginning to notice it. Then, as we began to get used to his condition there were times when we wanted to laugh – I did, anyway – but we couldn't. Maggie and Bernard were still too distressed. It wouldn't have been right. But this morning the ice broke. He was playing with Bernard, making little attacks on him and racing off down the corridor. On one of his sudden charges he tripped over a spare sleeping bag that was lying by the door. He hit his head as he fell but instead of complaining he launched himself at the sleeping bag and got into a mock battle with it, tossing it in the air and chasing it all around the complex.

It was Maggie who laughed first and that gave the rest of us permission. There has been loads more laughter since. There's no denying the seriousness of what has happened to him, but there's no denying the truth of what we've seeing, either. We know what he has lost but he doesn't. He has no idea what we're doing down here and he doesn't care. The fact is, like it or not, he's happier than any of us.

Because we're all bored stiff. We cook, we eat, we wash up and tidy up and after that there's nothing left to do except take turns on the computer and play games of cards. And listen to Radio Fightback, of course. Which is on 24/7.

The people of the village had no armbands, no icons, no torques, no tattoos. Some wore their hair long, others wore it short. As Nessa and Farral approached them at the edge of the village, they came forward and offered their names, and their right hands. Nessa returned her name, but not her hand. Farral willingly gave them both.

The whole village appeared to be gathered there to welcome them, from the very oldest to the very youngest. The hard, cold wind made it difficult to hear each other speak, and it was clear that no one was eager to stay outside. But when Nessa was invited to join them all inside one of the houses, she hung back. She had never been inside a stone house before. The thought of crowding into one with two dozen unknown people appalled her.

One of the villagers, a girl of about Nessa's age who had given her name as Fliss, stayed with her outside the door. Nessa noticed that she appeared to be fascinated by her eyes.

'We're not Dogs,' she said. 'I know we might seem like them to you, but we're not.'

'What are you, then?'

'Just people,' said Fliss. Her hair was neither long like a Dog's nor short like a Cat's but somewhere in between.

Nessa lifted her hand to her own hair. This time she had not even noticed it growing. It was about the same length as Fliss's. Instinctively she clutched at the gold-framed icon on its thong. She was still a Cat, but she had, she realised, become very lazy about her prayers and rituals. They were suddenly vitally important to her. 'I have to wash,' she said.

Fliss went with her and helped her draw water from the well and pour it into a tall, clay jar. But as Nessa was about to take it away and find a quiet place to wash, Fliss said, 'Your eyes. The birds never told us.'

'Told you what?'

'They told us everything about the Dogs and Cats on the other side of the Deadlands but they didn't tell us that your people had eyes like that.'

'They don't,' said Nessa. 'It's rare. A few in every generation, that's all. We're . . .'

She stopped. She had been going to say that the Watchers are special; that they had been sent by Atticus to remind his children of his presence and his law, and to watch over them. But now she knew she didn't believe it. She had never believed it. Maybe that was why Farral had gone to such lengths to seek her out. Perhaps he knew that, deep down, she had always been open to his ideas.

'It's enough, though,' said Fliss. 'It's proof.'

'Proof of what?'

'Proof that your people really are the descendants of Atticus.'

She said the name too easily for one who had no right to it. Nessa put down the jar. 'What do you know about Atticus?'

'Not much,' said Fliss. 'Not about his life, anyway. We know all about his birth, though.'

'How? How do you know?'

Fliss's eyes shone with excitement. 'I'll show you, if my parents will let me,' she said. 'I'll take you and show you how the old world ended and the new world began.'

2009

Wednesday ~~Friday~~: March 20

Attention! ~~An unidentified space creature — an intelligent space creature is about to unleash a deadly virus.~~

~~To Whom It May Concern. It has come to my attention than an alien creature of unknown origin is about to~~

Urgent. I am a scientist in the field of genetic engineering. I have certain knowledge that a ~~virus that will~~ deadly virus ~~will be may already have been~~ is about to be released upon the population. ~~The virus will~~ Take immediate action! Stay indoors. Keep all doors and windows tightly closed. Isolate anyone who shows cold or flu symptoms for at least four days.

This is not a terrorist threat. This is not a hoax.

Bernard finished the tests this morning. His expression told us what he'd found out even before he opened his mouth.

'I don't know how you figured it out, Christie, but you're right. The missing link gene is gone.'

There was a long silence, during which I had to battle hard with my swelling head.

'Just because you were right about that doesn't necessarily mean you're right about the rest of the Yoke's plan. You might be, though. And if you are, we have to do something.'

'We are doing something,' said Tina.

'We are,' said Maggie. 'But what about the rest of the people in the country? On the planet?'

'We have to get the news out there,' said Bernard. 'Any ideas?'

'E-mail,' said Sandy.

'Yes, it has to be e-mail,' said Bernard. 'But who do we e-mail?'

'Everyone,' I said.

'Government departments,' said Danny.

'Radio and TV,' said Tina.

A shock ran through me. 'My mum and your dad, Danny.'

'What do we say?' said Maggie. 'It's going to sound very weird.'

'It is very weird,' said Bernard. 'We still have to try and convince people.'

Sandy went off to try and get an Internet connection. The rest of us set about trying to compose a plausible message. This book was the nearest bit of paper. Bernard grabbed it. I didn't dare object. That's why our message is written out up there. ↑ We know it's unlikely to have much effect, but we have to do something. Even if only a few people take us seriously.

Sandy eventually got a connection, but even as she was searching for websites which might have the e-mail addresses we needed, an item of news on Radio Fightback caught Bernard's attention. The reason he always has the radio on is that he's listening for anything that might be relevant, but I don't think any of us really expected to hear anything. The news was all as usual up to then. Food shortages, energy short-ages, the war in the Middle East, or what was left of it. It was the name Jodrell Bank that caught his attention.

He turned up the radio. We had missed the beginning of the item but we got the gist of it. There was an incident, presumed to be terrorist. The control centre at the radio telescope had been taken over – by who was not clear. Fighter planes were overflying it and special service troops were being brought in. The newscaster promised to keep everyone informed.

'It's happening,' said Maggie.

Bernard re-read the e-mail we had written and shook his head in despair. When she had gathered most of the addresses she was looking for, Sandy typed out the message and added, at the end, 'Jodrell Bank is only the beginning.'

The connection collapsed before we could send out the e-mails and it took us another twenty minutes to get online again. While we were waiting I sat down with Danny and we composed another message, longer and more personal, to our parents. I know they'll believe it. I know they'll act on it. All I'm hoping is that it will get there in time.

Nessa slept in a tree that night, but not before she had been persuaded to accept the hospitality of the villagers. She had forgotten what it felt like to eat so well. Bread that was neither Dog bread nor Cat bread. Cheese. A heavy soup of barley and peas. She had forgotten as well how it felt to sleep after a meal like that, and she didn't wake until well after dawn.

Brockle was waiting for her to open her eyes. 'They're queer folk, these,' she said, watching Nessa as she washed at a hillside spring.

'They're queer all right,' said Nessa.

'They're like Dogs in some ways,' said Brockle. 'But some of them go out hunting at night like Cats do.'

'Really?'

'Really. Except that they don't hunt in the forest. They hunt in the sea. They hunt for fish.'

'How can they hunt in the sea?'

'They swim like the fish do. I saw them myself early this morning. Coming out of the water as if they were sorry to leave it.'

When they got to the edge of the village Farral was waiting for them. Fliss was with him, and a young man whom she introduced as her brother, Oliver. She was, as she had been the night before, brimming with excitement and enthusiasm.

'Everything's ready,' she said. 'We're all packed.'

A few yards away three sturdy ponies, one laden with baggage, were grazing alongside Bob and Ginny.

'There's something they're determined to show us,' said Farral.

'So I understand,' said Nessa. 'But where are we going?'

'North,' said Fliss. 'Right up to the end of the world.'

part
twelve

2009

Thursday ~~Saturday~~: March 21

Sandy got another old radio working so we've had two of them on all day, one in the kitchen and the other in the computer room.

A kind of gloom has settled over all of us. Danny, who is always less prone to introspection than the rest of us, has taken on the job of keeping Colin entertained. No one else feels up to it.

It's awful, just waiting. We've had a few replies to our e-mails, some of them sarcastic, some downright abusive, and one or two that are so absurd we had to laugh. Some of the government departments obviously have auto-reply programmes. One of them sent us this:

Dear Mr Russell,

Thank you for your correspondence to this department. The minister is always interested to hear the problems and opinions of his constituents and he will attend to your message personally in due course.

But there was worse to come. During the afternoon folk music programme on Radio Fightback we suddenly heard our e-mail being read out. We cheered, but the presenter hadn't finished.

'We don't believe in cranks on this station,' he said.

'We're in the business of putting over the minority view. So we decided to contact some experts in the field of genetic engineering.'

'Oh, no,' said Bernard, under his breath.

'The first two experts we contacted had never heard of Bernard Russell. The third one had. She said he had published an article some years ago in which he claimed that, given a very small genetic modification, animals and birds would be able to talk. Since then, no one in the scientific community has heard of him.

'So make of it what you will, Fightback listeners. Stock up on the baked beans – if you can find any, that is. Lock your doors. Shut that sniffling toddler in his bedroom for four days and don't let him out, no matter how loud he shouts.

'As for the reference Mr Russell made to Jodrell Bank, we have the latest update on that situation. No one can say for sure what happened because the staff there have all been taken in for debriefing by the military. But an army spokesman has told a press conference that there would be no arrests. Reading between the lines, it looks as if someone on the staff got a few wires crossed. Or maybe a few screws loose.

'Anyway. On with the music.'

Maggie put a hand on Bernard's arm. 'What can you expect?' she said.

Bernard was laughing too hard to answer, but it wasn't the kind of laughter that makes you want to join in. It was the kind of laughter that makes you fear for the person's sanity and starts you off considering your own.

The brother and sister could not have been more different. Fliss was perpetually bubbly and talkative, whereas her brother, Oliver, rarely said a word. They were both silent on the subject of what it was they were going to find at the end of the world, but they were extremely reassuring. Whatever it was, it was quite safe. They had been there before.

The weather continued to be wet and windy, but it was at least mild. They followed well-maintained tracks all the way, which was a great relief to Farral, who was surprised to discover in himself a deep love of everything orderly, and to Bob and Ginny, who could relax more now that they did not have to concentrate perpetually on their footing.

The four riders spent a lot of their time exchanging details of their communities. Nessa and Farral were cautious in what they chose to reveal, but it seemed that Fliss and Oliver already knew a good deal about their societies. Some of it was untrue. They had been told that Cats spent all their lives in trees and never set foot on the ground, that Dogs kept grunts in barns like cattle and ate their young, and many other things, some possible, others less so. But most of what they knew was accurate. The birds, who were so rarely in communication with either the Cat or the Dog populations, had nevertheless managed to glean information about them, and had passed a lot of it to the people up here north of the Foul Land.

Nessa and Farral knew nothing about the others, but they soon put that right. Fliss talked willingly, answering any and all of their questions without hesitation. If the talking grunts had any secrets, they were adept at keeping them hidden. The only thing they would not talk about was their destination, and what it was they were all going to see there. That, Fliss said, would speak for itself.

They were farming folk, like Dogs, but they were also, as Brockle had observed, very attached to the sea. There were a few isolated villages inland where the forest had been cleared, but the party encountered very few people as it travelled northwards. Most of the population, Fliss said, was gathered around the coast within easy reach of the water. Neither she nor Oliver were swimmers. They didn't have the gift, she said, though many other people in her village did. They were the lucky ones. They slept by day as Cats did, and by night they fished for the communities. In the summer they swam with the merpeople who lived their entire lives in the sea but the land-locked folk, like her, never saw them.

Farral asked if they ever went to war with one another. They didn't, according to Fliss.

'What about your gods?' said Farral.

'We don't really have gods. Or if we do, I suppose they are the sun and the sea and the soil and the forest. Why should we fight over them? They don't have any favourites among us.'

Nessa and Farral chewed that over for a while, then Nessa asked Fliss whether her people had laws to guide them.

She didn't seem to understand the question. 'I think there is law somewhere,' she said. 'To settle disagreements. But I have never seen it.'

'Rules, I mean,' said Nessa. 'Guidelines to live by.'

'Trust,' said Fliss.

'Trust?'

'That's a kind of rule. If it wasn't, do you really think our parents would have allowed us to come out into the forests alone with you two?'

Friday ~~Sunday~~: March 22

Radio Fightback is saying that people all over the world have been reporting shadows moving across the night sky. Not ships or saucers or UFOs. People who have seen them all report them the same way. Shadows. They block out the stars or the moon for a moment and then they're gone. No one can say what shape they are.

Bernard says it's impossible. He says that spaceships just couldn't have got here that fast from anywhere, not even from inside our own solar system. But there is no conviction in his words. We all know the Yoke doesn't operate on the same principles as we do. The laws of nature and of physics, as we have come to understand them, aren't applicable to what's happening now.

The weather has gone weird as well. Storms and cyclones. Thunderclouds moving over parts of the globe that haven't seen rain for years.

Bernard sent another e-mail to Radio Fightback. It wasn't mentioned. There is absolutely nothing more that we can do.

They were two days on the road. One night they stayed in a village – all except for Nessa, who still could not bring herself to sleep inside one of those stuffy houses. The other night they camped on a wooded hillside, and early the following morning they arrived at the end of a long, narrow glen which stretched away towards the distant sea.

Fliss and Oliver led the way down the glen, along a heavily used road that skirted a large and well-established village. A short way beyond it they encountered a number of other people congregating in a clearing in the woods. A neat wall of cut stone encircled a big pile of stones and ancient, crumbling mortar. From somewhere in the middle of the pile, a thin column of smoke was rising.

The other arrivals were filing into the circle. Fliss and Oliver dismounted, and Nessa and Farral followed suit. They left the horses at the edge of the woods and joined the line.

'What is this?' asked Nessa.

'It's the old world,' said Oliver.

'What? That?'

'Part of the old world,' said Oliver.

'The fourth one,' said Fliss.

'Were there four of them?' asked Farral.

'There must have been,' said Fliss. 'This is definitely the fourth one, anyway.'

Their attention was distracted by some of the other visitors, who were intrigued by the insignia that Nessa and Farral were displaying. As they answered the torrent of questions they gradually crossed through the ruins and arrived at a place where a newly made wooden door stood open, revealing a rectangular hole in the ground. The company fell silent as they walked down into the hole, one by one.

'I'm not going in there,' said Nessa. But the others passed her by and went in. From the darkness below the ground, Farral called up to her, 'You have to see this, Nessa.'

Her hackles bristled, but her curiosity won out over her fear.

Tiny flames were burning in little pots of fish oil. The light they gave off was dim but more than enough for Nessa's keen eyes. Ahead of her the others were moving along a central passage-way. On either side were doorways, all with fresh plank doors, all of them closed except for one, which stood ajar at the end of the passage. A brighter light shone out from it. They followed the line of visitors as they filed into it.

Two people were sitting at a table. Each of them had a long feather in her hand, and they were scratching some kind of symbols onto clean, crisp sheets of stretched skin. On the table between them stood more of the little oil lights and a redder light glowed from a clay stove against one wall. The room was warm and dry.

'What are they doing?' said Farral.

'Writing,' said Fliss.

'What's writing?' said Nessa.

The line of people had formed a rough semicircle round the table where the artists were working. Oliver led the way round behind them and showed them another table. 'This is what we brought you to see,' he said. 'It's very old.'

Nessa had seen glass before and Farral had seen more of it; pieces often came up with the earth as the plough turned it over. But neither of them had ever seen glass in a clean, neat piece. It covered the top of a small, flat box. Inside it was a pile of something like big, square leaves, with a worm-eaten scrap of black leather on top.

'What is it?' asked Farral.

'It's the diary,' said Fliss. 'It's the story of the fourth world.'

'How can it be a story?' said Nessa.

'There are marks on all the pages,' said Fliss. 'We can't look at it because it's too old and it would fall to pieces. But every few years a new copy is made.' She turned round and pointed to a stack of shelves, all of them packed with things that looked to Nessa like blocks of leather.

'That's what the writers are doing over there. They're copying out the diary.'

Nessa had some inkling of what Fliss was talking about. The artists in her own community had symbols for some words; she had even learned to make one or two of them when she was younger. 'Can you make it out?' she asked Fliss. 'Can you tell the story out of the marks?'

'I can,' said Fliss. 'So can Oliver. There are people in the village who know writing. They are teaching us. We have already learned how to read it.'

Farral was still completely flummoxed by the idea.

'You'll understand,' said Oliver. 'We'll hear the diary soon.'

2009

The first Radio Fightback news of the day was mostly the same old stuff. War. Economics. A new opposition demand for an election. There were more reports of shadows in the sky after that, followed by the news that the heavy rain which had been falling over the whole country for twenty-four hours was gradually passing away and clearer weather was coming in from the West.

The government-controlled station gave over most of its news broadcast to various front-bench politicians justifying the fact that there would not be an election in the foreseeable future. Then there was a short item by an astronomer, giving a patently bogus explanation about how thin, rapidly moving clouds could easily give observers the impression of a shadow passing across the stars. After that there was a psychologist who explained how impressionable people were, and how one sighting of a mysterious shadow can lead to dozens, even hundreds more.

It was the ten o'clock bulletin on Radio Fightback that first hinted at the bad news. Employers all over the country were reporting an unusual number of people off work, sick. Half the radio volunteers were out as well, so we were to forgive them if the programming wasn't quite up to scratch. Most of the people were complaining of the same symptoms.

Headaches. Pains in their bones. High temperatures. The newscaster himself didn't sound too good, and there was a definite anxiety in his voice when he assured his listeners that there was no connection with the e-mail they had received from a disreputable scientist two days earlier.

We were all devastated. Colin couldn't understand what was going on, but he picked up on the mood, poor thing, and took himself quietly off to his bed. I knew it didn't make sense but I felt responsible for everything that was happening. If only I'd seen it coming earlier there might have been something else we could have done. An even worse thought, which I couldn't get out of my mind for ages, was that I had somehow created the disaster by the act of imagining it. But no matter how hard I worked at it, I couldn't imagine a way of stopping it.

In the midday bulletin a different psychologist came on, talking about mass hysteria. There were wicked hoaxers out there, she told us, and the ordinary mild cold symptoms that were so widespread around the country were a hysterical reaction to a natural, but entirely unfounded fear. If anyone had a headache, she said, they should take a couple of aspirin and carry on with their life.

Radio Fightback was a bit more honest, as usual. The newscaster admitted that he wasn't feeling well but that he was sure he would be all right and so would everyone else. There was another rash of panic – the few people who had money to spare were buying anything and everything they could get their hands on. Some shops had closed because they were emptied out. Others had closed before they emptied. The few private cars that were on the roads were all to be found queuing at petrol stations. It reminded him, he said, of the Good Old Days.

That took my mind back to the beginning. Where all this had started. The oil crisis, or the Pump Slump, as everybody calls it now. I thought about the time before I made that mad journey with Danny and Tina and Oggy and Darling, before I ever heard of the missing link gene. It had all led to this point. Were we in Fourth World to blame for what was happening? Not because I'd imagined it, but because we had been too curious? Should we have stayed put in Scotland and left the yeti alone? Should Bernard and Maggie have had more sense than to start messing around with genetics?

Maybe. Probably. I don't know. Would I turn the clock back, if I could? Thing is, I don't know if it's a privilege to be one of the only people who knows what's going on. Assuming the virus doesn't get us – and it still might – will I be better off the way I am, or would I be better off like Colin?

It's a stupid question. What matters is that we have, or Bernard and Maggie have, outwitted the Yoke. It lent us its intelligence and then tried to take it back, but it isn't going to work. Even if it does get us all down here it can't get the others. The virus didn't work on Oggy and it won't work on Loki or Roxy or Oedipus or the birds or any of the wild animals. The Yoke has left a remnant of itself behind and it will spread again, even if there aren't any people left. And who knows? Maybe the animals will make better use of it than we did.

The reading of the diary took place every day and went on from morning until night. When the visitors to the old world had spent as much time as they wanted in the diary room they were brought into another of the underground chambers to eat breakfast and rest for a while. Then, when everyone was ready, they went into the reading room.

It was smaller than the diary room, but equally snug and dry. Thick sheepskin rugs covered the floor and the congregation spread themselves out in comfort and got ready to listen. Only Nessa was ill at ease in the confined space, but when the first reader began, even she forgot where she was and became entranced by the words which reached out to her from another time, another world.

This diary was a brilliant birthday present from Maggie. My birthday was three months ago, but she could hardly give it to me then, so she saved it for when I got back from Tibet. It's years out of date, but I don't care. I'd say it's almost impossible to get hold of a current one, and as long as I can get the day right I don't care about the year.

People came and went throughout the day. Some lived nearby and just popped in for a while to hear some of the diary and to have a good look at the Cat and the Dog who had appeared in their midst. Some brought little gifts with them, or food and drink to share with the other visitors.

Nessa became so engrossed in the diary that these occasional interruptions irritated her. She had lost all awareness that she was suddenly quite comfortable doing what Dogs did: gathering in a crowd beneath a roof; behaving almost as if she belonged to a family.

Some of the words were impossible to understand, and although Fliss and Oliver did their best, in hushed voices, to explain them, it was clear that they only had the haziest of ideas themselves of what a computer or a jigsaw might have been, and no idea at all about other things like vacuum cleaners, TVs and freezers. But the story made enough sense without them and Nessa's attention was riveted. Even Bonnie, who had slunk in behind them, appeared to be entranced, especially when Loki or Oggy were mentioned. But when a pair of hounds came in during the late morning, one yellow and one black, she slipped outside with them and was gone for quite a while. When she came back she settled quietly at Farral's feet, but at the next break, when everyone got up to stretch their legs, she jumped up and fixed Farral with an earnest look.

'I'm not a hound,' she said. 'I'm a dog. Loki is a dog and Oggy is a dog. Not hounds. Dogs.'

'It's just an old word for a hound, Bonnie,' said Farral.

'No it isn't,' said Bonnie. 'It's just the right word.'

'Well, if you're a dog, what am I?'

'You're a person,' said Bonnie, licking him on the nose.

'What's Nessa, then?'

'Person, too. Two persons, one dog.'

When the listeners assembled again, a new reader took over. Nessa stretched and reclined again on the rug.

What a mess. What a mess. I haven't slept for two nights and I still can't sleep, I'm so scared . . .

Sunday ~~Tuesday~~: March 24

I don't want to write down the thoughts I've been
having about what might be happening out there in
the rest of the world. I know we've all been imagining
the chaos. No one wants to talk about it. I don't
really want to write any more at all. There doesn't
seem to be any point. I can't remember why I ever
wanted to do it in the first place - our lives seem so
meaningless in the scale of things. If the virus gets us
there won't be anyone left to read it. The animals
maybe, though none of them yet has taken to
reading and I can't imagine it, somehow. And even if
the virus doesn't get us the future is going to be
nothing like the past.

But I've got to do something. We all have too much
time on our hands and we're beginning to get narky
with each other.

We stayed awake last night listening to the radios.
The virus was the only news. Everybody had it, not
only in the UK but all over the world. The government
station kept playing the same tune. Don't panic. Take
aspirin and drink plenty of fluids. Stay indoors.
Medical teams had isolated the virus and were
working on a vaccine. Everything would be all right.
There was a lot of talk about striking back, even
though nobody seemed to have any proposals about
who or what to strike back against.

Radio Fightback had a herbalist on, who assured us all that there were common weeds in everyone's back gardens that would cure us all. They also ran an item on what would happen at the Sellafield nuclear reprocessing plant if the staff got too sick to run the place. They said that if the core went into meltdown the whole of northern England and southern Scotland would become uninhabitable for hundreds of years. They told us as well that the skies were full of fighter planes looking for something to fight. As time went on we heard reports of those fighter planes falling out of the skies as their pilots became too sick to fly them. Eventually, before it got too late, they were all recalled to base.

Even then, some of the radio commentators were beginning to mix up their words and lose their train of thought. By the morning it was worse. One by one the radio stations went off the air. Bernard surfed the wavelengths, picking up stations in French and Italian and various other languages that none of us could understand. They faded out as well. By mid-afternoon the two radios were worthless pieces of junk. There was nothing left for them to receive.

We know that the virus becomes inert after three days. We know that because none of us caught it from Colin, and we know that we won't, because the incubation period is clearly only a matter of a few hours. All the same we have decided to stay here for as long as the water and air hold out. I don't know how long that will be. It's already getting stuffy down here. The smell of fish never goes away. We're all sick of it.

Bernard said there are bound to be pockets of survivors. No virus that was ever heard of affected everyone in the population. Nobody answered him. None of us felt remotely optimistic.

2009

Monday ~~Wednesday~~: March 25

Maggie had a false alarm last night. It's obvious
Bernard's really worried about her.

2009

Tuesday ~~Thursday~~: March 26

I'm going up the walls with boredom and
claustrophobia. I can't get any SPACE!!! And the fact
that we don't know what's really happening up there.
We're all going demented.

2009

Friday: March 27

2009

Thursday ~~Saturday~~: March 28

We didn't notice ourselves getting drowsy and lethargic. We thought we were just depressed. But Darling was our tester; she served the purpose that the canaries used to in the mines. When they stopped singing it meant that there was poisonous gas around. When Darling stopped talking and started falling asleep all the time we realised we were in trouble.

One of us had to go out. It couldn't be Maggie. She's well overdue by now and isn't looking too good. It couldn't be Bernard either, because he had to stay around to be midwife. The rest of us cut the cards. I cut the two of clubs. Just my luck.

We opened the trap door and let the fresh air in the garage come in. It probably wasn't that fresh, really, since it would have been sitting there for days, but at least it was unused. It still had oxygen in it. When we started to breathe it we realised how dull and tired we all were, and everyone felt better straight away. Bernard dug out an old fan and got the air moving throughout the complex, and the fishy smell, for once, got thinned out a bit. After an hour or so it was time for us to put the second part of the plan into operation. From there on in I was on my own. What do you say when you don't know if you've ever going to see someone again? 'Goodbye' was too frightening.

'See you,' I said.

'See you,' they all said back. They shut the trap and I waited while they resealed it. Then I stepped out of the garage into the open air.

The animals were not only OK, they were hysterical with delight at seeing me emerge. I was nearly as bad. The pups had managed without their gruel – amazing how fast they've all grown, even President Globalwarming. We were all so excited and busy with hugs and licks and exchanges of news that it was quite a while before I remembered what I was doing there.

I am the canary this time. My job is to test the air. Twenty-four hours is probably long enough, but to be on the safe side I am to stay out for forty-eight. If I feel ill I have to give the garage key to Oggy and make him promise to hide it and not to give it to me under any conditions. In time, someone else will come out and get it from him.

It's quite an assignment. Funny, what you can imagine if you're waiting for it so anxiously. Is that the beginning of a headache? A twinge in my back? Am I hotter than usual? Do I always feel as cold as this?

I took my mind off it all day by concentrating on the animals and getting up to speed with what's going on. The birds report that they have noticed odd behaviour among people in the village but nothing along the lines of my worst fears; no savagery. There is more of that kind of thing among the dogs and cats here at Fourth World. They are all, with the sole exception of Oggy, firmly entrenched in two camps. There haven't been any actual fights but they are not co-operating with each other at all, to put it mildly. What the dogs catch is for the dogs. What the cats catch is for the cats. According to Oedipus the dogs tried to take over the whole house and put the cats out, but he and the others managed to secure the upstairs and have a permanent guard on duty on the landing. They are using Maggie's window, which opens onto the roof of the garage, as a front door.

Getting negotiations under way was good for me. It kept my mind off the virus and its effects on the rest of the human population. I cooked a meal for all the cats and dogs. There is no fish for once but there was a heap of eggs down in the henhouse – amazing considering the poor old hens haven't been fed for over a week – so I put some of them in the porridge instead. I succeeded, after much persuasion, in getting all the cats and dogs to eat together in the kitchen, but it was under sufferance and afterwards they separated off again and returned to their strategic positions.

I'm writing now because I can't sleep. It's no joke. I've practically sucked my way through the glass of the thermometer already.

Before it got dark I walked up the glen to see Roxy and some of the others. We went on up to the top of the hill and looked out over Bettyhill and the sea. It was very weird. You can never see all that much detail from up there anyway, but there was something uncanny about the scene. There was a bit of movement on the shore – a couple of people, I thought, but there was no way of telling what they were doing from there. And all the boats were just sitting on the tide, all quite still, and the water getting rosy from the setting sun. All those boats and no one will ever sail them again. Eventually they'll break free of their moorings and drift away to sea, I suppose.

It's always quiet up there on the hill. I don't suppose

it was any quieter this evening than any other day but it felt as though a terrible silence had fallen over the whole world. It reminded me of my dream about being up there with the yeti. And then I remembered the other dream; the one where the end of the world came bursting out of the trapdoor in the garage. Was that what had really happened? It felt like it. It felt as though it was all over.

2009
Sunday: March 29

Bonnie was fast asleep, sprawled full length on the sheep-skin. From the doorway enticing smells of cooked food were reaching the people still gathered in the reading room. A lot of them had already gone, and one or two more got up and left as the reader turned the page, unable to resist the waiting meal any longer. But Nessa and Farral were still hooked. Beside them, Fliss and Oliver were watching them closely.

Nessa could see that the book was almost finished. There was only one more page still to be read. And yet the thing she had been waiting so long to hear had still not been touched upon. It was all fascinating, every word, but she could not see how it could relate to herself and Farral or the Cat and Dog world south of the Foul Land.

The reader began again.

'I had left six people behind me when I opened the garage door and stepped out into the new world.'

part
thirteen

2009

Saturday ~~Monday~~: March 30

I had left six people behind me when I opened the
garage door and stepped out into the new world. When
my forty-eight hours were up and I went back there
were eight. The celebrations that greeted my return
were more than relief for those of us who had evaded
the virus. They were for the new twins, who would now
have a chance of making something of their lives in
the strange times that lie ahead of us all.

Now I understand why Maggie was so huge. She
never told us she was expecting twins, but then I
suppose we didn't ask. We all felt a certain amount of
ambivalence about her pregnancy. She and Bernard
had given us their promise that they wouldn't bring
any more experimental children into the world, but
they had been unable to resist; they had broken it.
We had never asked them what animal genes they
were introducing this time because all of us, particularly Sandy, considered the procedure unethical. The
children that were born had no choice in the matter
of their genes and might, like Sandy, end up feeling
awkward and estranged.

But now that the twins are here there isn't one of
us who would wish they hadn't been born. They're
absolutely beautiful, both of them. One of them has
dog genes. He's human-shaped but he has funny-
looking ears and lovely, glossy hair all over him. The

other one has cat genes. When I first saw him I thought maybe they hadn't worked, because he looked just like any other normal human baby. But then he opened his eyes. They're still blue, but Maggie says they'll probably go green, the way the kittens' will.

They're not human eyes. They're cats' eyes.

It took me a while to get over the shock of that, but it took me even longer to get over the stupid names they've given them. I tried to persuade Maggie and Bernard to change them, but their minds were already set on far more important things. So that's the way the names will stay. The cat twin is called Atticus and the dog twin is called Ogden.

'I think she's a Watcher,' said one of the guards. 'Look at her eyes.'

Nessa stepped forward and approached a group of the village elders, who were clustered together beneath a tree, looking on.

'I am a Watcher,' she said to them, 'and these people here are my friends.' She introduced each of them. 'Farral. Fliss. Oliver. If you and your people have any interest in making peace with your neighbours, then we have a story that you might like to hear.'

The elders exchanged glances. The one who spoke was very old; a warrior who remembered the last outbreak of hostilities all too well.

'What harm can a story do us?' he said.

T he reader closed the diary and took it with her as she left the room. The other listeners went with her, leaving the four young travellers and Bonnie alone. For a long time all of them were silent, staring at the even, red glow of the stove. Then Fliss said, 'That's why we were so amazed by your eyes, Nessa. They are proof that you really are descended from Atticus.'

'My tattoos,' said Farral. 'To make it look as if we still have hair. Like Ogden had.'

There was another long silence. Eventually Nessa took a deep breath, and in a voice that was thin with disappointment, said, 'They didn't come out of the ocean, then.'

'Our people say that they sailed away,' said Fliss.

'By sea,' said Oliver. 'To avoid the Foul Land. The melt-down. So in a way they did come out of the ocean.'

'Some people say they were banished,' said Fliss. 'Because they divided the gifted beasts in the new world.'

'They weren't gods,' said Nessa.

'Neither of them were,' said Oliver. 'They were people. Partly animal, but mostly human.'

'Brothers,' said Farral. He took out his knife and tested the blade with his thumb.

Wild thoughts flew through Nessa's mind. Had the truth unhinged Farral? Was he going to turn on them all now? Show his true Dog colours?

But when he raised the knife it was towards his own throat.

'Farral! No!' Nessa made a grab for the knife but he caught her hand and held it away. The blade slid under the torque and sliced easily through the heavy leather. Beneath it was a band of clean skin, untouched by the weather.

He ran his fingers over the tattoos on his arms; the intricate interlacings of black and red. For the first time, Nessa felt an appreciation for the artist who had done it. The resemblance to the silky hair of a dog was remarkable.

Farral picked up the hound's-tooth torque and examined it. 'Some of these teeth were worn by my grandfather,' he said. 'Some of them are even older. But it doesn't mean we are dogs. We never were dogs. We're people.'

He dropped the torque into the stove. Slowly, the thick leather began to blacken and burn.

Nessa took the knife from him and cut off her armband and her icon. Without hesitation she dropped them into the flames. 'I can't do anything about my eyes,' she said. 'And I can't do anything about my tattoos,' said Farral.

'It doesn't matter,' said Fliss. 'They don't make any difference to who you are.' She was holding out her right hand again, as she and the other villagers had done on that first day. Farral took it. This time, so did Nessa.

The Cat guards delivered the four strangers into the village. 'They were riding gifted horses,' one of them said. 'We made them wait in the forest.'

Children were already racing in from all sides despite the late hour. Their aunts and uncles held them back. None of them had ever seen a group as strange as this one.

Their hair was neither as long as a Dog's nor as short as a Cat's. They carried nothing with them, except for one, who had a package of some kind bound in leather tucked beneath his arm. None of them wore the emblems of their faith, though one had tattoos and another bore a stranger, less familiar sign.